Blaze™

Dear Reader,

Nothing makes me pick up a book faster than a reunited-lovers hook. I'm a sucker for those "first love" stories where the hero and heroine, who were meant to be together from the start—destined, even—find their way back to each other. And if the path is littered with longing glances, what might have beens and hot sex, then all the better!

Bennett Wilder is the ultimate womanizing bad boy—he's a little wicked, a little wounded and more than a little in love with cop Eden Rutherford. Eden has been burned by Bennett a couple of times, and after he breaks her heart for the second time, Eden retaliates by forming The Ex-Girlfriends' Club, an organization for all of Ben's hit-and-run romances. The last thing she expects is a stalker to start posting to their Web site message board. Then things get even more complicated when Ben Wilder moves back to town...and Eden is the one who has to protect him.

I love to hear from my readers, so be sure to pop by my Web site—www.ReadRhondaNelson.com. I blog daily about the bizarre happenings that make up my everyday life. Sample headings include "Whine About It Wednesday" and "Dear Muse, Could You Please Show Up?"

Happy reading!

Rhonda

The
EX-GIRLFRIENDS' CLUB
Rhonda Nelson

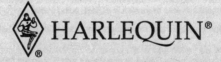

HARLEQUIN®

TORONTO • NEW YORK • LONDON
AMSTERDAM • PARIS • SYDNEY • HAMBURG
STOCKHOLM • ATHENS • TOKYO • MILAN • MADRID
PRAGUE • WARSAW • BUDAPEST • AUCKLAND

ISBN-13: 978-0-373-79326-6
ISBN-10:   0-373-79326-X

THE EX-GIRLFRIENDS' CLUB

ABOUT THE AUTHOR

A Waldenbooks bestselling author, past RITA® Award nominee and *Romantic Times BOOKreviews* Reviewers' Choice nominee, Rhonda Nelson writes hot romantic comedy for the Harlequin Blaze line. In addition to a writing career, she has a husband, two adorable kids, a black Lab and a beautiful bichon frise who dogs her every step. She and her family make their chaotic but happy home in a small town in northern Alabama.

Books by Rhonda Nelson

HARLEQUIN BLAZE

HARLEQUIN TEMPTATION

*Chicks in Charge
†Men Out of Uniform

Don't miss any of our special offers. Write to us at the following address for information on our newest releases.

Harlequin Reader Service
U.S.: 3010 Walden Ave., P.O. Box 1325, Buffalo, NY 14269
Canadian: P.O. Box 609, Fort Erie, Ont. L2A 5X3

For the makers of Butter Rum Life Savers,
Crunch 'n Munch, Reese's Peanut Butter Cups,
Super Bubble, Stride Gum and
Diet Mountain Dew, without which this book
would not have been possible.

And to Pudd'nhead,
whose charming personality inspired Cerberus.

Artemis525: I'm thinking someone needs to break *Bennett's* heart. *Literally.* Like maybe snatch it from his chest, then run over it with a lawn mower. <BEG>

EDEN RUTHERFORD READ the new drive-by post and felt another nudge of unease prod her belly. Granted she was still a bit of a rookie on Hell, Georgia's, police force, but even a rookie could discern the somewhat unsettling menace behind this most recent message. She instinctively picked up the cordless to call Kate, her best friend and cofounder of the Ex-Girlfriends' Club, but the thought was interrupted by the ringing of the phone. A quick check of the caller ID confirmed that Kate had beaten her to the punch.

"Did you see it?" Kate asked gravely.

"I did," Eden told her, equally unsettled. And annoyed, dammit. The board was their cyberspace playground and this weird chick was kicking sand. "I was just about to call you."

Kate released a worried breath. "This woman is really starting to freak me out, Eden. *Run over his heart with a lawn mower?* Sheesh. She's got issues. I seriously think we need to consider banning her from the board."

The same thought had occurred to Eden, but she wasn't even certain it was possible. Granted the sole purpose of the Web site and message board was to bash Bennett Wilder—or any other man who employed his hit-and-run style of romance—but this…

A huge proponent of the old you-reap-what-you-sow adage and justice in any form—be it poetic or otherwise—Eden still thought *this* fell smack-dab into over-the-top territory.

Quite frankly, after all the heartache he'd heaped upon her and the rest of her little club, Bennett having a broken heart in the *figurative* sense would be particularly gratifying. She inwardly snorted. Hell, he'd certainly left a lot of casualties in his wake—most notably *her,* Eden thought.

But *literally* was out of the question.

Or at least it was to all of Bennett's victims but one.

Artemis525 had started posting to the board a couple of weeks ago—which was strange in and of itself—and there'd been something about her even then that had given Eden pause.

Though the site was dedicated to Bennett, within a couple of months after it had gone live, their cathartic vengeful-humor sort of therapy had served its purpose, and now the site was more about lamenting daily woes: problems at work, meddling mothers—usually hers, Eden thought with a mental eye roll—PMS and the occasional Mr. Wrong. Having a broken heart courtesy of Hell's third-generation bad boy might have been what had originally gotten them together, but it certainly wasn't what kept the group talking now.

That's what made Artemis525's posts so strange. Despite the fact that she seemed to have materialized out of thin air, they hadn't even been discussing Bennett. Hadn't in months.

Without warning, dark brown hair, even darker heavily lashed old-soul eyes and lips a little too full to be anything short of sexy materialized all too readily in her rebellious mind, making a melancholy tide of longing rise up inside her. Tall, hard and lean with a smart mouth, a smoother tongue and a smile that epitomized wicked, Ben Wilder should come with a warning label. After all this time, the mere memory of him could still cause her foolish heart to jump into an irregular rhythm and a hollow, woeful ache to appear in her belly. Eden released a small breath.

Bennett might have left town three years ago, but there was rarely a day that went by that she didn't think about him. Pathetic? Eden rolled her eyes. Without a doubt. Despite considerable evidence to the contrary—particularly where Bennett was concerned—she wasn't stupid.

But…Eden couldn't seem to help herself.

In fact, to her immeasurable shame and chagrin, she'd *never* been able to keep her wits about her when it came to Bennett, a fact that became glaringly evident with each botched attempt at resisting him. He crooked his finger, she came. The end. The emotional tug and off-the-charts attraction she'd always felt for him had never been governed by anything remotely close to rationale. It had been ruled by her heart and her body, completely excluding her brain and anything close to common sense.

He was Bennett—*her Ben*—and, as such, he would always hold a special place in her pathetically miserable broken heart.

Though he'd been a good kid, an A-plus eager-to-please—almost *desperate*-to-please, in retrospect—student and a budding athlete through the majority of their school years, something had happened to Bennett in their senior year of high school, and for no apparent reason he'd done an about-face.

For starters, he'd dumped her—right before prom, which at the time had been the mother of all humiliations—without reason, without provocation and without warning.

She'd been devastated, and to this day Eden still didn't know why he'd done it.

Then his grades had plummeted, he'd started hanging out with the wrong crowd and within a month had become their ringleader. Most painful of all, he'd turned into a skirt-chasing fiend bent on bedding practically every girl in the county.

In short, the seemingly manic effort he'd put into toeing the line—a misguided attempt to atone for the bad reputation of his parents, she knew—had been nothing compared to the effort he'd put into *crossing* it.

He smoked. He drank. He cursed. He grew long hair and pierced his ear. Tame by regular standards but positively scandalous in their little hometown. A strange set of rules for a city named Hell, of all things, she'd admit, but just as rigid as any Bible Belt burg below the Mason-Dixon Line.

And the first time he'd tossed one of those heavy-lidded, baby-I-could-rock-your-world glances at her, she'd *melted.*

She'd fallen hook, line and sinker. Eden let go a shallow breath.

But Bennett Wilder had the rare ability to make a girl feel as though she were the only woman on the planet, and more importantly, the only one for *him* in the entire galaxy. When he'd looked at her and smiled—*just smiled*—the rest of the world had simply fallen away. Eden grimaced.

Unfortunately, being with Bennett meant that her world was in danger of being rocked, flipped, shattered and otherwise knocked for a loop and off its axis.

Prior to his move to what she'd dubbed his dark side, they'd been high school sweethearts. The term sounded so blasé, so casual—unsubstantial, even. And yet even now Eden couldn't competently describe what that time—every minute spent with Ben—had meant to her.

Holding hands, planning futures, building dreams while she watched him whittle away on a piece of wood. He'd been funny, earnest, dark and sexy and, though she hadn't realized it at the time, curiously grateful for being with her. She smiled sadly, remembering. He'd been her hero, her warrior, her confidant and best friend. And on a hot summer night by Fire Lake, he'd been her first. She'd been his, too, which for Eden had made it all the more sweet.

Call her stupid, but even after all this time and even knowing what she knew now—that years later they'd get back together and he'd dump her *again* without so much as a goodbye—she still believed that they'd had something special.

Regardless, that second breakup had been particularly hard to swallow. Four years at Georgia Tech followed by three in Atlanta as a probation officer had given Eden seven years' worth of distance and perspective…which had promptly fallen by the wayside the minute she'd returned to Hell at twenty-five.

Come home, her dad, Hell's longtime mayor, had pleaded. *Hell needs you.* More like *he'd* needed her, but Eden had been homesick all the same. She hadn't necessarily missed her mother, who sadly she'd never been close to. But she'd missed her aunt Devi—her mother's sister and surrogate mama—and all the people of her little town.

Just as she'd feared, though, she hadn't been back in the apartment above her parents' garage two weeks before she'd been right back in Bennett's bed. Time hadn't changed a thing. The pull, the need, the absolute unadulterated desire to be with him had been stronger than ever.

He'd been working construction for Ryan Mothershed at the time, and she'd happened upon him at the Ice Water Bar and Grill. An hour of playing pool and a single slaying glance later and pre-dictably—*poof!*—her panties and her good sense had both fallen away. Given his particular talent for making her brain and her undergarments disappear—not to mention his own penchant for vanishing from her life—Eden had secretly dubbed him "the Magician."

The only thing that never actually managed to fade was the way she felt about him. That, Eden thought with a tired smile, was purely magical.

She'd tried dating a bit while in college and later, working for Fulton County, but nothing had ever compared to the way Ben had made her feel. Sure, she could develop a certain fondness for other guys and drum up a bit of sexual enthusiasm, but it was barely more than superficial, and ultimately Eden had given up the business altogether. Other than the requisite ricochet lay after Bennett had left town three years ago, to help soothe her wounded pride, Eden hadn't been with anyone since.

Her mother was constantly harping on her to find someone new, get married and produce some grand-children, but Eden had decided those things simply weren't in her cards and she'd come to terms with that. Did she long for a family? Sometimes get lonely? Of course. But settling wasn't worth it, and she enjoyed her own company too much to compromise.

"Do you think we should let him know about this woman, Eden?" Kate asked, thankfully detouring her unproductive walk down memory lane.

Eden blinked, jarred back into the present. "Let him know about it?"

"Yeah," Kate said. "Something's not right."

Eden rubbed an imaginary line from between her brows, tried to gather her focus, which was hard anytime her thoughts drifted to Bennett. She agreed that something wasn't right, but the idea of contacting him didn't feel right, either.

Distinctly wrong, in fact.

As far as she knew, Bennett had left town for good immediately after he'd left her bed and had put those woodworking skills he'd learned from his grandfather—Grady Wilder, another rounder, Eden thought with a fond smile—to very profitable use as an artisan catering to the Low Country's upper crust.

Despite everything that had happened between them, Eden secretly warmed with pride at his success. She was equally proud of him and for him. She'd always known that he had a special talent, and seeing that recognized and knowing how validated it must make Bennett feel was especially gratifying.

By all accounts, he'd created a life as far removed from Hell as possible. Thanks to Kate, she was aware of his monthly treks to the Golden Gate Retirement Home to see his grandfather, but as far as she knew, he'd never darkened another door in town aside from that one.

Thankfully, and much to her shame and ultimate relief, Eden hadn't seen him again.

Certainly there were times when she fantasized about what she would say if she ever ran into him. What girl who'd had her heart broken didn't? But the idea of willingly contacting him after he'd walked away without so much as a goodbye had never occurred to her.

Eden considered herself relatively brave—she had to be in her line of work—but facing Bennett required an emotional courage and a sexual wherewithal she wasn't altogether certain she possessed. In fact, past history had consistently proved otherwise. So her best course of action if she wanted to hang on to her heart, her underwear and the smallest modicum of self-respect demanded that she stay far, far away from him.

Furthermore, she had too much pride and, frankly, didn't know whether she could get through the confrontation without breaking down and making a fool of herself. She swallowed.

True, he'd broken her heart in high school. But three years ago, when he'd walked away for the second time, he'd *obliterated* it.

She had no one to blame but herself, of course. *Fool me once, shame on you. Fool me twice, shame on me.* But knowing that certainly didn't lessen the hurt. It only served to make her feel more stupid. In retrospect, giving him the second chance—the "by," as Kate had called it—hadn't been the wisest move she'd made, but per tradition, she hadn't been able to resist and…she'd still believed in him.

In *them,* specifically.

And she'd been wrong.

The Web page had been her bitter brainchild, her way of injecting a little retribution toward Bennett, even if it had been conducted through the somewhat passive-aggressive venue of cyberspace. It had made her feel better—all of them, as a matter of fact. Just because she'd been the most recent casualty didn't mean that the others' heartbreak had been any less.

"Eden?"

She started. "Er…do you really think it's that serious?" she asked Kate. "Serious enough to contact him?"

"Don't you?"

"I don't know," Eden said, knowing as the words left her mouth that they were a lie. Kate was right. Something about Artemis525's post stirred her instincts, and those instincts told her that the woman— whoever she was—didn't appear to be wired correctly.

But did they need to call him? Warn him? Honestly, so long as he wasn't in town she didn't see any reason to alert him to the threat. Between the psycho's local ISP address—meaning she was using a local Internet service provider—and Bennett's reputation, she felt as if this chick was a hometown girl. She shared her opinion with Kate.

"What do you think?" she asked, hoping against hope that her friend wouldn't call her on being a coward, an agonizing label which set her teeth on edge.

Aside from Bennett, she'd never been afraid of anything in her life.

Kate paused, then let go a breath. "I guess you're right. But I'm going to let the other nurses know to call me if I'm not on shift the next time he visits Grady." A significant chuckle drifted over the line. "I'll let him know about her."

Eden chewed the smile lurking at the corner of her lip. "So you're going to tell him about the club?"

"I'll have to, won't I?" Kate replied, sounding particularly pleased with the idea. Though Kate hadn't been a Bennett casualty per se, she'd been there to nurse Eden through her heartbreak. At an even five feet, with short dark hair and pale blue eyes, Kate was small but fierce. Like Tinkerbell, Eden had often thought.

Eden grinned, somewhat heartened by the idea that Bennett—whom she was relatively certain didn't know the site existed because she hadn't felt the wrath of his anger pinging her from Savannah—was going to find out what she and the other girls had done. A perverse thrill whipped through her imagining his handsome outraged face.

"Think he'll ever move back here?" Kate asked conversationally, a question that had been widely speculated, debated, otherwise mulled over and betted on since his swift to-hell-with-all-of-you departure.

Ha, Eden thought as her lips slid into a rueful smile. "Maybe when Hell freezes over."

And considering how quickly she and her brain and various items of clothing tended to part company anytime he came around, that was soon enough for her.

2

Welcome to Hell.

Population 7,958 and growing. The only thing hotter than our hospitality is our barbecue sauce!

A broken laugh erupted from Bennett Wilder's throat as he read the sign heralding his hometown's city limits. Now that was apt, he thought darkly. It might not be the literal eternal hereafter for the damned, but it might as well be the equivalent to him. His fingers involuntarily tightened on the steering wheel and he bit back a blistering curse.

He still couldn't believe he was coming back here. Couldn't believe that he'd finally found his place in the world, made his mark and now... Bennett expelled a weary breath.

As though the devil himself had a hand in his fate, he'd been lured back to Hell, Georgia, the last place on the globe he wished to visit, much less live. In all truth, nothing short of a hot poker applied to his ass could have brought him back, either—and even then it would have been a hell of a fight—but one call for help from his grandfather had been all it had taken to make a liar out of him.

I'm sorry, but he has to go, Bennett, Eva Kilgore, the director at the Golden Gate Retirement Home, had told him two weeks ago. *He's a pip, I'll give you that. But he's simply too...disruptive. Relatives who encourage their loved ones to live here expect what our brochures advertise. Peace, harmony and well-being. Since your grandfather moved in, we've had none of those. He's organizing protests against the menu. He's fleecing everyone out of their pocket money at the card tables when we've repeatedly told him that gambling for cash—or change—* she'd emphasized sternly *—is forbidden. And that's only the minor infractions.* She'd blown out a disgusted breath and shaken her head. *Frankly it's the womanizing that's turned this home into a circus. We can't have the women getting into catfights over your philandering grandfather during movie hour, Bennett,* she'd said. *It's not good for them. Not good for anybody.*

No amount of pleading, flattery or even bribery had convinced Eva that she shouldn't kick Grady Wilder out of the retirement home. Since Golden Gate was the only facility in the county, it had left Bennett with no options. Even if Grady would have been willing to move into nearby Willis County, Bennett wouldn't have had the heart to make him.

Hell, for better or worse, was his home.

So here Bennett was, moving back after three blissful years away from the poisonous gossip and grueling grind of being the bastard son of two of Hell's most notorious citizens. Kathie Petri, his mother, had been a teenage drifter who'd migrated from southern Louisiana to Hell without parents, without money and without morals. His father, Kirk Wilder—whose own mother had died during childbirth—had been a local boy, but a bad seed. So the two of them hooking up had been as disastrous as it had been inevitable.

Bennett had learned the hard way that no matter how much effort he put into being an upstanding member of the community, he'd never successfully shirk the weight of his parents' mistakes. He'd always be "that Wilder boy."

Could he help it that he'd been born to a couple of low-life misfits who hadn't been fit to own a pet, much less raise a child? Was it his fault that his mother had been a shameless whore the other women had shunned? His father a mean, shiftless, jealous drunk? A perpetual embarrassment to the community?

No.

But that didn't matter because here in Hell his parents' drinking-whoring-fighting legacy would always be a shadow he couldn't shake. Thanks to an unpleasant and ultimately life-altering chat with Giselle Rutherford—the mayor's wife and the

mother of the only girl he'd ever cared about—
Bennett had realized that at eighteen, but hadn't
had sense enough to accept it until he was twenty-
five. That's when he'd cut and run, leaving his
grandfather and the only girl he'd ever considered
a…friend…behind.

Friend couldn't begin to describe what Eden
Rutherford had been to him, but anything more
than the casual label made his skin feel too tight for
his body. Made his palms sweat and his mouth
parch. Made him wish that he'd fought for her rather
than taking the path he'd chosen.

*You are nothing and will never amount to any-
thing,* Giselle Rutherford had told him. *Less than
the trash your parents were. And I will not permit
you to drag my only daughter down with you. You
say you love her?* She'd sneered as though he were
incapable of such an emotion. *Prove it. Because
every time she sees you, I'm going to punish her.
And it will be your fault.*

At eighteen, Bennett hadn't known what to do,
had felt powerless to fight back. And he hadn't
doubted for a minute that her mother would make
good on the threat. He'd witnessed too many of her
spiteful reprimands, most notably when she'd destroyed a wooden heart he'd carved for Eden. *The
bitch,* Bennett thought now, remembering how devastated Eden had been. He'd known at that point
that she'd be better off without him, and though

it had almost ruined him, Bennett had caved to Giselle's threat.

With no other choice available, he'd broken up with Eden and had given up any pretense of trying to be good enough to make up for his parents' reputation. He couldn't be, he'd decided, because his good would never been good enough. Not by Hell's standards. By the time he and Eden had gotten back together years later—no longer intimidated by her, he would have as soon told Giselle to kiss his ass than look at her—he'd realized that, in taking that path, he'd unwittingly fulfilled her mother's condescending prophecy. He'd become the very nothing she'd said he would be.

In what could only be described as divine punishment, he hadn't made that realization until Eden had told him that she loved him. That's when he'd left town and made a new life for himself. His insides twisted with bitter humor.

He had Giselle Rutherford to thank for that, if nothing else.

Regardless, the mere thought of Eden made his gut clench, his heart ache and his dick invariably stir behind his zipper. Kind but fierce green eyes, a soft, slightly crooked smile that promised as much mischief as pleasure and an easy yard of hair as pale as a moonbeam.

In a word: *gorgeous*.

And if Hell had royalty, she'd be it. She was a

true Hellion, Bennett thought, smiling in spite of himself, and the label fit on more than one level.

The only daughter of the perpetual mayor—which was not unusual in the South—and his ultimate bitch of a wife, Eden had grown up in a relatively loving home. Her father had loved her, at any rate. Her mother didn't appear capable of loving anything but an appearance and, as such, had made Eden's life a living hell.

Despite that, however, she'd been a straight-A student, a cheerleader and choir girl—odd hobbies for a tomboy, but that was Eden—and from the moment she'd shared her apples and cheese with him in the second grade when he'd arrived without a snack, he'd viewed her with equal amounts of suspicion and awe. She was sweet but feisty, with a strong sense of fair play and a penchant for acting first and thinking later. From the time they were small she'd had the unique ability to make him feel like something other than a contaminated outcast. Bennett frowned.

Years later, of course, things would take a romantic turn and she would make him feel something much more substantial and altogether more frightening, something that would ultimately make him ashamed of himself, would drive him out of town and into his new and improved life.

And it was new and improved, dammit, if occasionally empty. But better empty than *here*, Bennett thought, feeling the familiar niggling of inadequacy erode his self-confidence as he drove farther into town. God, he hated it here. Hated how he felt when he came here.

In Savannah he was Bennett Wilder, sought-after artisan. He'd built furniture for some of Hollywood's A-list, for pop stars and politicians. He attended all the right parties, could pick and choose his dates—not that he'd bothered much—and enjoyed all the perks of being a local celebrity of sorts. Nobody cared who his parents were or where he came from. It was refreshing, had been like being reborn and coming out *right* this time. He'd dusted the red dirt off his feet, had made regular monthly visits to his grandfather and had moved on.

Or as on as he could without Eden in his life.

Did he want to live in Hell? Be looked down upon once more? Feel the suspicious stares of the local folk? No.

But that was only the half of it.

Knowing that he was going to be living in the same town as Eden Rutherford and knowing that she could never be his was infinitely worse—his *real* hell on earth.

Bennett had known when he'd walked away the last time that he was permanently severing ties, though at the time he'd never anticipated seeing her again.

Which, admittedly, made things quite difficult now.

He couldn't move back here and *not* see her. Even keeping the lowest profile possible, Bennett knew he'd inevitably run into her again. And when that happened…well, who knew what would happen? Would she slap him? Certainly possible. Frost him? Another option. The only thing he knew for sure—could count on as well as the sun rising in the morning—was that he'd want her again. Ha! As if he'd ever stopped. He'd want her with the same all-consuming, blinding need that inevitably struck him whenever he saw her. Bennett chuckled darkly. Not wanting her was like commanding his body not to breathe. Likewise, not having Eden was about as successful as him holding his breath indefinitely.

A moot point.

Eden had always been his kryptonite, his downfall, his saving grace and his ultimate weakness. For both their sakes, this time he was going to have to be stronger than the attraction, stronger than the emotion that never failed to twine around his heart and make him long for things he knew weren't in his future. A wife, a family… Nah. He'd let those things go when he'd walked away last time, as well.

Frankly, being flayed alive and dipped in boiling oil held more appeal than moving back to Hell, but there was simply nothing for it. Bennett might have been an out-of-control teen, might have made multiple stupid youthful mistakes, but he was man enough to repay his debts—and he owed Grady Wilder.

The old man had been the only constant in his life, the only person who'd stood between him and a foster home when his parents had perished in a house fire. He'd been eleven at the time. Just old enough to understand that their lives didn't remotely resemble the families on TV, the beginnings of shame rounding his usually bruised, too-thin shoulders.

Too much to drink, a careless cigarette…a fiery end to their equally combustible lives.

A mail carrier with a penchant for minding everyone's business—retired now, of course; a fact that the citizens of Hell no doubt appreciated—Grady had been there. Ornery, obstinate and a bit on the eccentric side, but he'd loved Bennett all the same, and that had made the difference. Just knowing that someone had given a flying damn about him had made living seem as though it wasn't a complete waste of time. *Come on, kid,* he'd said. *Let's go home.*

And that had been that.

He'd moved in, had learned that it was okay to speak even if he hadn't been spoken to. That spilled milk wasn't going to land him a backhand across the face and that outgrowing his clothes wasn't a cause for punishment. He'd learned that a good work ethic and honesty made the backbone of a man—a fact his father had missed though they'd both ultimately been raised by the same man. And most importantly he'd learned that, with patience and creativity, a block of wood could become a beautiful thing. Bennett swallowed.

Damn straight he owed Grady Wilder. And while returning to Hell might not have been on his top-ten-things-to-do list, he'd do it anyway.

After a lot of blustering and roaring, Grady had finally agreed to let him renovate the house and the barn. *Speaking of which...* Bennett thought, reaching for his cell phone. He needed to call Ryan Mothershed—his previous employer, his soon-to-be contractor and the only friend he'd kept in contact with since leaving Hell.

He and Ryan had forged a friendship on the gridiron which had survived despite Bennett's abrupt enrollment into Badass 101 after high school, as well as his subsequent move out of town. Ryan had participated in a foreign exchange program to England during college and returned with more than a degree—he'd brought back a wife, as well. Bennett often teased him about successfully transplanting an English rose in Hell. They had a little boy—Tuck—and another baby on the way.

"Mothershed," Ryan answered by way of greeting. Bennett could hear various saws buzzing in the background as well as the hydraulic whoosh of a nail gun firing.

"I just rode into town," Bennett told him.

"That explains it."

"Explains what?"

"The collective gasp of horror from the old biddies I heard echo through the streets."

"Smart-ass," Bennett groused, chuckling. "So have you looked at your schedule and figured out when you can get started on my renovations?"

The house needed a little TLC and some updated wiring to competently hold what would be his second office, and the old red barn would house his new shop. In the meantime, there was a small shed in the backyard that would accommodate him. It's where he'd started, after all. He'd hired movers to transport his must-haves, and barring any unforeseen problems, he should be back on track by the end of the week. In truth, Bennett could have done the majority of the renovations himself, but he simply didn't have the time. A good thing, he told himself, whether Grady agreed or not.

"I can have a crew out there Wednesday," Ryan said. He shouted an order to someone in the background, then swore under his breath. "I just thought you might need a little time to talk Grady around."

"Done," Bennett told him.

"He's completely agreed? He isn't going to give me any trouble?" The last time Ryan had worked for Bennett's grandfather, repairing a section of the front porch, Grady had positioned his rocker within a foot of the crew for optimum critiquing power. Needless to say, it hadn't been a positive experience for his friend.

"He knows that the work has got to be done if I'm going to stay here."

Provided he had the right space, he could work here just as well as in Savannah, he'd assured Grady, who'd immediately given up any pretense of wanting to live alone.

The fact was he simply wasn't able. Hip replacement had corrected the majority of his physical problems, but getting around was still a chore. Add his failing sight to the mix and he was an accident waiting to happen. Bennett didn't think Grady needed round-the-clock care, but another warm body in the house would go a long way toward his peace of mind.

Initially Bennett had tried to talk Grady into moving in with him in Savannah, but he might as well have been asking Thomas Jefferson to trade places with George Washington on Mount Rushmore for all the good it had done. His grandfather had been every bit as solid in his reserve. *Hell's not a bad town,* he'd said. *You'll see when you come back. Perspective changes things.*

Bennett didn't know about that, but he did know one thing. He *would not* allow anyone the privilege of making him feel like a second-class citizen again. He'd done a lot of growing up over the past three years, knew that he'd given everyone in Hell plenty of reason to treat him like the bad seed he'd tried to live up to as a bitter kid, and later, as a bitter adult.

But he'd changed, and the difference between the

old Bennett Wilder and the new one was simple—he liked himself now. Screw 'em if they didn't like him. Other than making a few late-in-coming apologies—particularly to Eden, he thought with another mild grimace—he didn't owe them anything. He was who he was. They could either accept him or not, but it wasn't going to change his attitude or the purpose of his moving home. Grady deserved better. Hopefully he could simply slip back into town and become part of the scenery. Blend in. Keep it low-key. Be unremarkable.

That was the plan, at any rate, inasmuch as he had one. Only time would tell if it would come to fruition.

"You want to meet up at Ice Water tonight?" Ryan asked.

Bennett knew what his friend was doing and appreciated the show of support, but shook his head. "Thanks, but no." Walking back into Hell's infamous watering hole—the gossip hub of the community—the first night he was back in town didn't coincide with his keep-a-low-profile plan.

"All right," Ryan told him. "I'll see you Wednesday morning then." He paused. "Happy to have you back, man."

Then that made one of them, he thought grimly, but thanked his friend anyway and disconnected.

Welcome to Hell, my ass, Bennett thought. He damned sure wasn't expecting anyone else to be happy with his return.

3

"DO YOU KNOW WHAT THAT son of a bitch said to me, Eden?" Josie Brink screeched as she aimed a loaded .22 rifle at her quivering husband's privates.

Eden rounded the hood of her patrol car and released a weary sigh. "No, I don't, but you can tell me after you've put the gun away. You know better than this, Josie. Don't make me call the chief. I'll look like an idiot, and you know he promised to take that rifle the next time you threatened to emasculate your husband."

Josie blinked and shot her a questioning glance. "Emasculate?"

"Shoot his dick off," Eden clarified.

Understanding dawned and she nodded, then her eyes narrowed into angry slits once more. She cocked her head. "Yeah, well, after I shoot his sorry ass, I won't need the gun no more, will I?"

And there was that, Eden thought, trying desperately to summon patience. This had been the day from hell. Jeb Wheeler had once again been on his cross crusade, stealing the little white memorials which had been placed on area roadsides by loving family members in honor of accident victims.

For reasons no one could explain, Jeb would periodically troll the roads, steal the little wooden crosses and install them in his front yard. Evidently he thought they made fetching lawn ornaments. *Jeb's pulled his little Arlington again,* was the usual call that went out over the radio.

Eden had spent the majority of the day convincing Jeb to give up the crosses—she was the only person who'd ever successfully talked him into giving them up, which is why she *always* got stuck with the call—then returning them to their rightful owners. She'd had less than an hour to go on her shift when this call had come in.

As the only woman on the force, she generally got any calls the guys dubbed "girl trouble." Sexist? Yes, but given Josie's current state of mind, Eden couldn't imagine any of those tactless oafs she worked with being able to handle this one, either.

"Come on, baby," Neal Brink cajoled his wife. "I was only kidding. Can't you take a joke?"

No, stupid, Eden thought exasperatedly, a fact Neal apparently hadn't deduced yet. But in Josie's defense, Neal's "jokes" were rarely funny. Neal, the twisted little jerk, liked to play his jokes on his wife during sex. The last time Eden had been called out here, Neal had been in the middle of an intimate service for his wife, looked up from between her legs and said, "Not as sweet as your sister's, but it'll do."

Predictably, Josie had Katie-kaboomed, and it had taken Eden the better part of an hour to talk her out of doing permanent injury to her husband. God only knew what he'd done this time, Eden thought, and tonight she wanted nothing more than a cool beer from Ice Water and a steaming plate of hot wings. Thanks to Jeb, she'd missed lunch, and it was beginning to look as though Neal's twisted sense of humor was going to screw her out of a reasonable dinner.

Eden glared at Neal. "Judging from that rifle pointed at your family jewels, Mr. Brink, I don't think Josie finds your jokes funny." She looked at Josie, who seemed heartened by Eden's support. "What did he do, Josie?" she asked, calling upon every shred of patience she had left.

Josie shifted, causing the spaghetti strap on her pink nightie to slip off her slim shoulder. "Remember what he did last time? What he said about my sister?"

Oh, hell. "I do," Eden replied, blasting Neal with another withering stare.

"Well, he did sort of the same thing, only this time he looked up at me and said—"

"Mmm, mmm. Tastes like chicken," Neal finished with relish, then dissolved into a fit of guffaws that made Josie's finger snug dangerously close to the trigger.

Eden gasped and covered her mouth to prevent a rebellious giggle from escaping.

"See!" Josie screamed. "See what I have to put up with? He's not sorry! He doesn't care that he's hurt my feelings!"

"Baby, how many times do I have to tell you that it was a *joke?*" He laughed at her and shot Eden a look that said his wife was evidently lacking a sense of humor. If that was the case, then Eden was lacking one as well because she probably would have murdered him by now.

Josie fired a shot at the ground at his feet. A clump of grass flew up and hit him in the shin. The smile quickly vanished from Neal's lips, and his eyes widened in fearful horror. *"Woman, what the hell are you doing?"* he gasped.

"Excellent shot," Eden commented with an impressed nod. She wasn't worried about Josie killing him. If she'd wanted to do that, she would have done it already. Furthermore, Neal deserved Josie's *joke*.

Josie discharged another round, this one at a hanging plant next to Neal's head. Potting soil and hot-pink petunias flew, showering him in a dirty spray. *"Playing a joke, Neal,"* she said sweetly. "Isn't it funny? Ha-ha!"

Neal's outraged gaze swung to Eden as he batted a torn bloom from the top of his head. "What kind of law officer are you?" he demanded. "Are you going to let her keep shooting at me?"

"That depends. Are you going to stop playing jokes on her?" She crossed her arms over her chest and leaned casually against her car.

"And he's got to apologize, too," Josie piped up, flipping her hair away from her face. She raised the rifle once more, narrowed one eye and took aim. "'Cause if he don't, he's gonna be *real* sorry."

"I'm sorry!" Neal shrieked when it was evident that Eden didn't intend to intervene on his behalf. "Dammit, woman, I'm *sorry!*" He let go a shaky breath. "Sweet Jesus, just put the gun down."

Josie considered him for a moment, then looked at Eden. "What do you think?"

He sounded more terrified than repentant, but as an officer of the law, she wasn't supposed to encourage violence…whether she thought it was justified or not. "I think if he's smart, he won't play any more jokes on you during sex."

Josie nodded. "No more jokes, Neal," she ordered through gritted teeth. "Understood?"

He shoved a shaky hand through his thinning hair, dislodging more potting soil and flowers. "Understood," he said weakly. "Sheesh. Women."

Seemingly satisfied, Josie walked over and handed Eden the rifle. "You'd better take it. I'm not so sure I won't really shoot him if there's a next time." Hell, Eden wasn't so sure *she* wouldn't shoot him if there was a next time.

She grinned, accepted the gun and stowed it in

the back of her car. "You could always leave, you know," Eden felt compelled to point out. Honestly, looking at the two of them, she'd never understood the attraction. Josie was a pretty girl, if a little rough around the edges. She could certainly do better than Neal Brink.

"Nah," Josie said with a small wistful shake of her head. "He makes me laugh." She turned and started to walk away, then lowered her voice and shot Eden a conspiratorial smile. "And it doesn't hurt that he's hot in the sack."

And on that note, it was time to leave, Eden thought as her mouth rounded in a silent *oh* of revolted surprise. She could have happily gone the rest of her life without that little kernel of insight about Neal Brink.

Furthermore, there was something distinctly depressing about the fact that Neal Brink, despite being of relatively limited intelligence and appeal, was married and getting laid more often than she was.

Eden sighed, slid behind the wheel and welcomed the cool blast of air that hit her face as she negotiated the rutted dirt driveway. Only May, and yet the temperature had to be a humid ninety degrees. Summer was undoubtedly going to be a scorcher, which would ordinarily make Southerners moan and groan, but not where she lived. In fact, the city council would be thrilled. Eden felt a small smile curl her lips. After all, they hadn't renamed the city Hell for nothing.

Originally the town had been named after Colonel Jamison Hale, a Confederate commander in the Civil War who'd ultimately settled their little parcel of land in South Georgia. But for reasons that meteorologists had never been able to competently explain to the citizens of her little burg, this particular area had boasted record heat for more than one hundred and fifty years. Deciding that they should capitalize on the phenomenon in order to attract tourists, city leaders—namely her grandfather, who'd been mayor right up until his death, which was when her father had stepped in—had adopted Hell in favor of Hale. And the rest, as they say, was history.

Despite its eternal-hereafter-for-the-damned name, Hell was a good city. Fine, hardworking people lived and raised their families here. And due to the surprisingly busy tourist trade, it had evolved into a hip mecca of sorts for those who'd become disenchanted with big-city life. Naturally they got their share of Goth visitors, but the town was small and had a lot to offer. She rolled to a stop at the intersection and relaxed against the back of her seat while she waited for a break in late-afternoon traffic.

In order to be of better service to her community—and because she loved the science and technology of it—Eden had enrolled in CSI, or Crime Scene Investigation, classes at a nearby college. Just because she lived in a small town didn't necessarily mean they had to act like one.

Eden knew both of her parents had been happy when she'd moved back to town. Her father had actually asked her to come home—to be the buffer between him and his wife once again, Eden suspected—and her mother had been happy to have Eden to criticize once more. Then again, what else was new? Eden had never been the meek, stain-free, angelic little automaton her mother had wanted. If there was a fight, chances were she'd started it. A mud puddle to jump in? Both feet. She'd worn her dresses with a mutinous face and snatched the ribbons out of her hair the minute she'd left Giselle's line of vision. She'd always befriended and dated anyone she chose, despite her mother's protestations, and done things her own way regardless of the consequences. Eden frowned.

And there'd been many.

Fewer now that she was adult, of course, but her teenage years—especially when she'd been dating Bennett—had been sheer hell. One instance in particular still stood out, possibly because in the end it had been so prophetic.

In a routine act of blatant defiance her father thankfully ignored and which only served to infuriate her mother, Eden had snuck out to be with Bennett. They'd cruised the back roads in his old truck, doing a bunch of nothing—which, of course, had meant everything to her. He'd carved a wooden heart out of a piece of peach wood while they'd sat on his tailgate, then attached it to a piece of fishing line he'd found in the back of his truck and given it to her.

Much like the illusion necklaces that were popular today, it had hung as though by magic, suspended directly over her heart. He'd tied the charm around her neck, then kissed her cheek and told her that he loved her. It had been the first time he'd ever said it, and Eden had gotten so choked up she hadn't been able to return the sentiment for several minutes.

Naturally her mother had been furious upon Eden's return, but she'd been floating on a cloud of happiness, bouncing along on a current of endless joy because Bennett Wilder had loved her, and she hadn't paid Giselle much attention.

The next morning the necklace had vanished from her dresser, and she'd found it lying splintered next to her breakfast plate.

That's what he's going to do to your heart, anyway, her mother had said with a cold, unrepentant shrug. *If you leave this house without permission again, I'll make you even sorrier than you are right now.*

In that moment, Eden had hated her mother more than anything in the world and had never been more thankful for her aunt Devi, whom she'd cried to later. However, as though her mother had had some sort of psychic connection, Bennett had broken up with her shortly thereafter.

Eden swallowed, forcing the memory away. The

breakup had been bitter enough without having to endure her mother's smug I-told-you-so expression.

While Eden knew her mother enjoyed her position as the mayor's wife, she'd nevertheless always gotten the impression that it had never been quite good enough. It angered her on behalf of her father because, in her opinion, he deserved so much better. Eden had always had an exaggerated sense of fairness—of right and wrong and people being treated accordingly. It was no small part of the reason she'd gone into law enforcement. Her lips twisted with bitter humor.

Unfortunately there was nothing fair or even about her parents' marriage—her father did all of the work and her mother reaped the benefits.

In the end, though she might moan and groan about some of her less interesting calls on the force, Eden was quite happy with her career. Hell had always been good to her, and while she might miss the occasional trip to the museums and her season tickets to the Braves games, Atlanta had never truly felt like home. Hell, with its slow pace, perfectly manicured square and eccentric personality, was home. She enjoyed being a cop, being out in her community. Leveling the playing field. Serving. Protecting.

Eden's eyes narrowed as a black BMW flew past. Like protecting people from that idiot, she thought as she darted out behind the driver and hit the blue lights. Good grief. At the rate she was going, she was never going to get that beer. Or the hot wings. Annoyed, she hit the siren, as well, and felt a perverse jolt of pleasure when the driver pulled off to the shoulder of the road.

She eased in behind the car, radioed dispatch to let them know she'd made the stop and calmly snagged her ticket pad. Georgia tag, she noted as she made her way to the driver's-side window, but she didn't think it was a local. She didn't recognize the car, at any rate.

The fine hairs on Eden's neck prickled as an achingly familiar profile suddenly registered in her rapidly numbing brain. Sound receded. She looked down and her gaze tangled with a pair of dark, sexy—equally shocked—eyes. The air suddenly thinned in her lungs, and her palms and feet tingled with an electrical current that, by all accounts, should have made the ground quake.

After all, it made everything inside her vibrate.

Eden swallowed, felt her blood pressure rocket toward stroke level, her mouth parch, her empty belly roll. Oh, dear God.

Bennett Wilder was back. Her lips slid haltingly into a bitter smile.

Evidently Hell *had* frozen over.

4

PULLED OVER. FABULOUS. Just freakin' fabulous. Less than five minutes back in town and he was already in trouble with the law.

Swearing under his breath, Bennett pushed a difficult smile into place and turned as the sound of crunching gravel grew ever closer. "Good afternoon, Offi—"

The rest of the sentence died in his mouth as recognition broadsided him. If he hadn't been sitting down, he would have staggered under the weight of emotion that suddenly slammed into him.

Though her cap hid her hair—her most remarkable feature—there was no mistaking those wide green eyes, that pert nose and lush mouth. Nor the faint half-moon scar on her chin, a product of an early encounter with the edge of a coffee table as a toddler, if he remembered correctly.

And he knew he did, because everything about Eden Rutherford was memorable.

And just to make absolutely certain he recognized her, a firestorm of heat blazed behind his zipper, the same blistering, thought-singeing wave that had always let him know he'd gotten too damned close to her. Need ripped through him so fast it tore the breath from his lungs, making him momentarily unable to speak. So much for keeping a low profile and keeping a distance, Bennett thought, feeling himself inexplicably lean toward her.

Eden.

"Hi," he said for lack of anything better.

"Bennett," she replied coolly, despite being obviously jolted at seeing him again. Her pulse fluttered wildly at the base of her delicate throat, and he discerned the slightest tremble in her smoky voice. God, how he'd missed her. "This is a fifty-five-mile-an-hour zone. You were traveling ten miles per hour over the limit."

"I know," Bennett admitted, considering her with equal parts joy and trepidation. Unable to help himself, he offered a smile. "Sorry about that."

Rather than return his grin—much less acknowledge that they'd been infinitely more than mere passing acquaintances—she looked away and consulted her ticket pad. "Is there any particular reason you're in such a rush?"

Was this an official question or was she fishing for information? Bennett wondered, foolishly hoping for the latter. Given the tone of her voice, there was really no way to tell. Odd, that, when he used to be able to read her so well. "Actually, I'm heading out to Golden Gate to pick up Grady."

A concerned frown emerged between her brows, and the first hint of the real Eden appeared behind her official cop demeanor. "Oh? Is something wrong?"

"Physically? No," he quickly assured her, then he checked his watch and winced. "At the moment, he's probably packed up, sitting curbside on his luggage and pissed that I'm not there yet."

"Packed up? Where's he going?"

"Home," Bennett told her. "He's, er…" He paused, felt an uncomfortable smile tug at the corner of his mouth. "Let's just say he's no longer a welcome resident at the retirement home."

Eden gasped, reluctantly intrigued, he could tell. "Eva kicked him out? I knew she'd threatened to in the past, but I can't believe she actually went through with it."

Bennett nodded grimly. "Believe it."

"Why?"

"Oh, a combination of things," Bennett said lightly, hoping to thaw her a little with humor. It had always worked in the past, after all, he thought, his gaze inexplicably drifting over the smooth line of her cheek. "Inciting revolts over the menu, gambling, not respecting the curfew." He sighed, tapped his fingers against the steering wheel and stifled a grin. "But ultimately it was the womanizing that Eva couldn't tolerate. She said it was unseemly."

Eden didn't smile, but her eyes twinkled. "I'd heard about that."

From Kate, Bennett thought, remembering that Eden's best friend was a nurse on staff at the retirement home. On the rare occasions their paths crossed, she never failed to send him a death-ray glare.

Eden frowned thoughtfully. "I didn't think Grady was able to live alone anymore."

"He's not," Bennett confirmed. His gaze tangled with hers and he shot her a distinctly uncomfortable smile. "I'll be living with him."

Blind panic—which made him feel like the biggest dick in the world—surfaced in that too-green gaze before she managed to blink it away. "O-oh?" she asked, clearing her throat. "What about your work? I'd heard you were doing quite well in Savannah."

"I can work from here as easily as I can in Savannah," Bennett said, pleased that she'd been keeping up with him. The only fly in the ointment of his recent success was that he hadn't been able to share it with her. When it came to his woodworking, Eden had always been his biggest fan. "I'm keeping the store open there but will do the physical end of the job here."

"From your grandfather's?"

"Yeah," Bennett confirmed. "I'm renovating the house and barn. The barn will be my shop."

Eden waited for a line of cars to pass before

speaking again. The blast of hot air tugged at a loose strand of hair hovering distractingly around her mouth. "Aunt Devi bought one of your rockers the last time she was in Savannah."

He actually remembered Eden's eccentric aunt coming in. *Devi Darlaston,* he thought. God, what a character. While Eden's mom had always been cold and calculating, Devi had been a sweetheart, a grounding support for Eden. For whatever reason, she'd always reminded him of his grandfather. She'd chosen one of his favorite pieces, too—a rocker he'd crafted from oak, its back an intricate design of corkscrew willow branches.

"I hope she liked it," Bennett said, hating himself for fishing for the compliment.

"She did." Eden considered him for a moment, seemed to thaw just a bit. "It's beautiful work, Bennett."

The remark made a warm dart land in his chest and expand. He'd received countless praise for his work, and yet, for whatever reason, her opinion counted more than any other. Then again, it always had. "Thanks," Bennett murmured, swallowing.

Eden released a small breath, inadvertently forcing his gaze back to her ripe mouth. Just looking at it brought back snapshots of kissing her, stuck on fast-forward.

The first time, at her locker, and she'd tasted like butterscotch candy.

At her back door—they'd broken apart guiltily when her mother had turned the porch light on.

Fire Lake, their first time, and he'd softly pressed his lips to hers—an apology for that brief flash of pain he'd seen in her gorgeous eyes as he'd carefully slid into her.

Heaven, Bennett thought now. The only time he'd ever felt *right.*

With his eyes Bennett traced the woefully familiar lines of her face—that hot mouth—and felt both his heart and his loins catch fire. Like a match to dry tinder, his entire body went up in flames, scorching him from the inside out. His fingers involuntarily tightened on the steering wheel, and he swore inwardly, praying for an instant downpour to put out the blaze. He watched Eden's suddenly heavy gaze drop to his mouth and felt himself harden to the point of pain.

Motherfu—

He couldn't do this, Bennett thought, setting his teeth against the tide of longing rising up inside him. Hadn't he promised himself that he wouldn't do this? He didn't deserve her, and more importantly, he couldn't hurt her again.

For both of their sakes he had to stay away from her. There was too much at stake. Grady needed him…and Eden needed him to leave her alone.

As if coming out of a trance, Eden blinked and an awkward smile caught the corner of her mouth.

"Well, I don't suppose I should write you a welcome-home ticket, so this time I'll just give you a warning."

Bennett's lips edged into a grateful smile. "I appreciate it. Thanks."

"See you around," Eden said. Then, after a slight unsure pause, she turned and walked away.

That was exactly what he was afraid of, Bennett thought. He couldn't afford to see her around. Because he'd do something stupid they'd both ultimately regret.

EVERY CELL IN HER BODY vibrating with nervous adrenaline, Eden slid back behind the wheel of her car and waited for her racing heart to slow. Her mouth was so dry it felt as if she'd eaten a pack of chalk. Her palms were numb, her fingers tingled…and yet her nipples were hard. She looked down, snorted miserably and shook her head.

This was what Bennett Wilder did to her. What he'd always been able to do to her.

Barely three minutes in his company and she was a *wreck*.

Jeez, God, did he have to be so damned handsome? Eden silently lamented. Was it too much to ask that he develop some sort of deformity or at the very least a serious skin problem since the last time she'd seen him? She let go a stuttering breath.

Evidently so, because he looked better than ever.

His dark, wavy hair was shorter than he'd worn it previously, and rather than keeping traditional sideburns, he'd trimmed his into the trendy edgy look she'd seen favored by hip urban professionals. If possible, they made him look even sexier. More dangerous. Hell, Eden thought with a miserable chuckle, he could have trimmed them into a fleur-de-lis pattern and he still would have looked like a badass.

Because that, in essence, *was* Bennett Wilder.

Eden sighed. And therein lay the attraction. Or at least some of it. Frankly, for her, there'd always been more to Bennett than his sex appeal. He was smart and interesting and talented and vulnerable. He had *fix me* written all over him and she'd tried to do just that three years ago and had gotten her heart filleted for her trouble.

Now that was not a mistake she'd be making again, Eden thought, glad that—other than that one little please-get-out-of-the-car-and-kiss-me moment when she'd been mesmerized by his mouth once again—she'd mostly kept her wits about her.

She waited for him to pull out into traffic, then dropped her head against the steering wheel and moaned with a combined cocktail of mortification, misery and self-disgust.

This was not good.

At least she hadn't cried or ranted like a madwoman, like the proverbial scorned lover. She'd kept her cool, kept it relatively professional—she hadn't been able to resist asking about Grady or telling him that the rocker was beautiful. But ultimately she'd kept her head, which was nice considering it felt as if it had momentarily left her shoulders the instant she'd looked into those dark, brooding eyes. Eden knew he'd expected her to go off on him like a Roman candle, and there was something quite gratifying about the fact that she'd managed to surprise him.

Furthermore, the minute she'd found out that he was moving back here permanently, she really should have given him a heads-up on Artemis525. She'd started to but then had ultimately chickened out. How did one begin that conversation, anyway?

By the way, Bennett, after you broke my heart, me and some of your other exes started a Web site designed with the express purpose of maligning your character. One woman in particular seems to really hate you and wish you harm. Frankly she gives me the creeps, so you might want to watch your back. (Insert uneasy laugh.) Welcome home.

Ha. She didn't think so.

Kate had volunteered to be the bearer of that news, not her. And as luck would have it, Kate was on duty and Bennett was on his way out to the retirement home. Talk about karma. Eden picked up her cell and dialed her friend, hoping that she'd be sitting at the nurses' desk.

"Golden Gate, your home away from heaven," Kate's weary voice came across the line.

"Thank God," Eden replied, relieved.

"Eden? What's wrong?"

"You're never going to believe who I just stopped."

"Bennett?"

Eden gaped and felt her eyes widen. "How did you know?"

"Because Grady has been going around all day telling everyone that he's moving out, that Bennett's moving back and that Eva is a disciple of Satan." She blew out a tired breath. "And not necessarily in that order. I had planned to call you, but as you can imagine, things have been crazy here. Grady's friends threw him an impromptu going-home party, and somehow or other, several bottles of Southern Comfort were smuggled in. Drunk senior citizens, walkers and electric wheelchairs don't mix, Eden," she said darkly. "Believe me, it's bad. Bad, bad, bad."

Eden chuckled, imagining. "I'm sorry."

"Let me guess. You're calling me to give me the four-one-one on Bennett so that I can relay the four-one-one to him on Artemis525?"

Eden surveyed traffic, then aimed her car back onto the road. "You know me too well."

"Coward," Kate teased, rightly pegging her.

Yes, she was. And an ultimate fool, because seeing him again had energized her in a way that she hadn't felt in a long, long time. One look into those old-soul eyes had knocked her so far into the hot zone again that she hadn't been able to think straight, much less think cattily. She'd just been proud of herself for not completely losing it.

"We'll need to call a meeting," Eden told her, trying with difficulty to focus. And the first order of business would be what to do about the Web site. She didn't want to shut it down, of course—and didn't intend to—but keeping it up and running under BennettWilderSucks.com with him moving back to town felt…off to her. Had he softened her that much already? Eden wondered, analyzing her motives. Or, all things considered, was it the prudent move?

"How are we going to do that without tipping off the crazy chick?"

Good question, Eden thought. "I don't know. Maybe call everyone?"

"That's assuming this isn't someone we see every day."

Right again, but she simply couldn't imagine that being the case. Then again, stranger things had happened. Many a murdering freak had appeared normal, right? "I guess that's a chance we'll just have to take. I'd still rather call than post it."

"You aren't afraid he'll see it, are you?"

"No," Eden told her with more force than was actually required. "I hope that he does." And she did. He'd hurt her—hurt them all. If seeing their embittered musings and uncharitable thoughts made him a bit uncomfortable, then so be it. It was nothing less than he deserved. This would be a sentiment which would undoubtedly require many reminders, Eden thought grimly. She'd just seen him and already she could feel her grudge withering away. God help her if he apologized. Instead of game on it would be game over, and she knew it.

Kate chuckled with gleeful relish. "Oh, to be a fly on the wall."

She wouldn't mind finding a little wall for that one as well, Eden thought, her lips curling at the idea.

"You take care of getting everyone together and I'll take care of bringing Bennett up to speed," Kate said, practical as ever.

"Eight o'clock tonight at my house sound okay to you?"

"Sure."

"Come early," Eden told her. "And bring booze. *Lots* of booze."

Knowing what was to come—the draining buzz and hoopla surrounding the return of Bennett Wilder—she was going to need some sort of alcoholic assistance.

5

"IT'S ABOUT DAMNED TIME," Grady snapped predictably as Bennett rolled to a stop beneath the portico. "I could have died waiting on you to get here."

"And yet you're well enough to complain," Bennett replied with a droll sigh.

Eva Kilgore, every steely gray hair pinned into submission, stood with stoic resolve next to Grady and seemed particularly relieved that Bennett had finally made an appearance. He nodded a greeting at her. "Eva."

"Bennett," she returned with cordial chill. "He's ready."

And so am I hung unspoken in the air.

Grady glared at Eva, his dark eyebrows furrowed in deep contrast with his snowy hair. "It was only a little going-away party, you old stick-in-the-mud. You just *had* to ruin my fun right up until the very last minute, didn't you?"

Bennett hit the remote to open the trunk and paused, a finger of unease tightening his gut. He slid a cautious look at the pair of them.

"Your *fun* is precisely why you don't have a home here anymore, Grady Wilder," Eva shot back, her thin lips pursed into nonexistence. "It's a miracle no one had a bad reaction to that alcohol."

Grady chuckled softly, a hint of Wilder wickedness evident in that small laugh. "Oh, I think they reacted to it the way they were supposed to."

Bennett smothered a long-suffering sigh and arched an eyebrow at his grandfather. "Alcohol?"

"Harmless," Grady pshawed.

Eva's nostrils flared with disapproval. "Reckless," she countered darkly. "Minnie Winston is lucky she only dislocated her hip when she fell, and didn't break it."

"Minnie hadn't had anything to drink," Grady said. His dark brown eyes twinkled and he shot Bennett a wink. "It was the weed that knocked her for a loop."

Eva gasped, her eyes widening in horror.

"Oh, for pity's sake, woman," Grady said with put-upon exasperation. "I was only kidding."

Wearing a look of determined consternation, Eva shoved a clipboard at Bennett. "Sign these and he's all yours."

"Yeah, sign those and get me out of this hellhole. The Queen of Darkness here can have it," Grady mouthed off, eyeing Eva with beady distain.

"Behave," Bennett warned Grady in a low voice, signing where she'd indicated.

Eva snorted under her breath. "Good luck making that happen."

Bennett gestured toward the single suitcase at Grady's feet and arched a confused brow. "Is this it? Where's the rest of your stuff?" Bennett knew for a fact that Grady's room had been outfitted with a TV, a DVD player and a laptop computer—he'd bought them himself—not to mention the movies, games and books.

"He held an auction last night," Eva announced with smug chagrin before Grady could respond.

Bennett passed a hand over his face, torn between exasperation and irritation, both of which were commonplace to anyone who dealt with his grandfather on a regular basis. "You sold your stuff?" he asked in a carefully neutral voice.

"Less for you to lug in," Grady told him, blushing slightly, his gaze darting away. "I was doing you a favor."

"Oh, well. So long as you were thinking of me," Bennett replied, tongue planted firmly in cheek. He easily loaded the suitcase into the trunk, then waited until Grady had settled himself into the front seat before closing the door for him.

Bennett looked at Eva and smiled sheepishly. "I'd say it's been a pleasure, but…"

"Oh, no," Eva said, her voice ringing with belated joy. "The pleasure has been all mine. Good luck," she said grimly. "You're gonna need it."

"Bennett!" Looking tired but relieved, Kate Manning hurried through the front doors toward him. "Can I have a minute?"

Eva darted a curious look at Kate but merely raised an eyebrow and turned and walked away. If it hadn't been unseemly, Bennett imagined she would have skipped.

Intrigued but uneasy, Bennett nodded. He and Kate had never had what one could call a friendly relationship. She'd tolerated him for Eden's sake when they were dating, but he knew, given how he and Eden had parted ways, those days were over. Not that he blamed her, of course. He'd been a cowardly ass.

Bennett had picked up the phone half a dozen times to call Eden and apologize, but to his un-ending shame and self-loathing, he'd never been able to muster the courage. She'd want an explana-tion, Bennett knew, and that was where things were going to get sticky. He'd never told her about her mother's threat—dreaded making the cowardly ad-mission—and he'd ended things between them the last time before she could ask him about it. She'd probed a little, of course, but it had always been too easy to distract her with more feel-good pursuits—as in, making love to her.

He'd planned on tendering the ridiculously too-late-in-coming apology, but honestly, he hadn't planned on her being the very first person he'd see the minute he rolled back into town. Did he intend to man up and make it? Yes. He just needed to find the right moment to do so.

Grady rapped impatiently on the window. "What's the holdup?"

"Give me a minute, would you?"

"At least turn on the air," Grady snapped, scowling. "I'm roasting in here."

Oh, for the love of— Bennett opened the door and handed his grandfather the keys. "Crank it up. I'll only be a minute."

His grandfather smiled pleasantly at Kate, transformed, as usual, at the sight of a pretty girl. "Ms. Manning."

"We'll miss you, Grady," Kate told him. Unlike Eva, who'd been relieved, thrilled and otherwise beside herself to see Grady leave the retirement home, Kate seemed sincere. Evidently she appreciated his grandfather's particular brand of charm. The idea made him smile.

"What can I do for you?" Bennett asked Kate.

"Nothing," she said, crossing her arms over her chest. "I just wanted to give you a friendly warning."

Bennett looked away and inwardly swore. Pulled over and now a "friendly warning." So far he'd been back in town less than thirty minutes and already he could feel his hair-trigger temper itching. He deserved this, he knew. He'd hurt her friend. Naturally she was concerned that he would do it again and now she was going to warn him away. Though it chafed, Bennett couldn't blame her. This was all part and parcel of owning his past mistakes, so rather than tell her to go to hell, Bennett steeled himself against the impulse and stood there, determined to do the right thing.

"Look," he said, rubbing a hand over the back of his neck. "If this is about Eden, I—"

"It is and it isn't," Kate interrupted. "Here's the thing. After you left, Eden and a few of your other ex-girlfriends got together and formed a club of sorts."

What the hell—an ex-girlfriends' club? Bennett thought, stunned. He cleared his throat, unsure of what to say. "My ex-girlfriends formed…a club?"

"Yes," she confirmed. "With a Web site. You should check it out," she said sweetly. "It's www.BennettWilderSucks.com."

BennettWilderSucks.com. How…nice, Bennett thought, absorbing this little bomb and congratulating himself for keeping his cool. He could do this, Bennett thought. He could be nice. Though there was nothing to smile about, Bennett felt his lips slide into a pained grin.

"Anyway," Kate continued. "It should come as no surprise that the women who visit the Web site aren't exactly *fans* of yours—"

No, that definitely wasn't a surprise, Bennett thought darkly.

"And there's one woman who's been posting for

the past couple of weeks that we thought we might need to give you a little heads-up on." Kate winced, though Bennett could tell that she was ultimately enjoying herself. "Her remarks are a bit…disturbing."

Bennett wasn't quite sure where to start. "Disturbing?"

"Yes. Eden's concerned. We suspect that it's a local girl and so long as you weren't here we didn't feel like you were in any danger." She pulled a shrug. "Now that you're returning to Hell permanently, we thought that we should let you know."

"We?"

"Eden and I. We founded the club and the Web site, though I have to admit it was Eden's idea. BennettWilderSucks.com," she reminded him unnecessarily with another patently false smile.

"Right," Bennett said, shooting her a grim look. "I got that part." He'd just seen Eden, though. Why hadn't she told him? Bennett wondered. No wonder she'd panicked when he'd told her that he was moving back to town permanently. Aside from the obvious reason, of course. Furthermore, no doubt she didn't want to tell him that her little joke had resulted in him being the object of a threat.

"I don't know what you've done to Artemis525, but she's not posting any of the typical Bennett's-a-womanizing-bastard stuff. She's more interested in doing you physical injury."

Excellent, Bennett thought with a humorless

laugh. *Just excellent.* Life in Hell wasn't going to be hellish enough. Now he had a hate club, a hate Web site and a crazy unknown woman wanting to do him physical injury.

This was the Hell he remembered.

His grandfather chose that moment to lay on the horn, startling both of them. Bennett's grim gaze swung to Grady.

And he'd be living with the devil incarnate.

Seemingly finished with her civic duty, Kate let go a happy breath. "Anyway, just wanted to let you know, bring you up to speed. Probably you should watch your back. And if anything bizarre happens, then definitely report it."

Right. And who would he tell? Eden? He snorted. Wouldn't that be ironic?

Because he knew she wouldn't expect it and because he was grimly determined to keep a cool head, Bennett summoned a smile and thanked Kate for the information.

She paused—predictably startled—and considered him for a lingering moment. "Take care of Grady," she finally said, albeit suspiciously. "He's a sweetheart."

Not what he would call his grandfather—who, evidently in boredom, had decided to start rifling through his glove compartment—but Bennett didn't argue.

"What was that all about?" Grady wanted to know when Bennett finally joined him in the car.

"The usual Hell welcoming committee," Bennett said grimly as he pulled out from under the shady portico. He sighed and darted a look at his grandfather.

Deep lines marred a face that had once held a stronger jaw and a slight slump rounded wide shoulders Bennett had often admired and relied upon. His hands were still just as large, but age and arthritis had withered away some of the strength. The scene was eerily familiar, but seventeen years ago it had been in reverse. He'd been the smaller, needier one. And Grady Wilder had come through. Bennett swallowed. "Let's go home," he told Grady.

And that, as it had been for him—hate club and crazy chick or not—was that.

6

"WELL, I JUST CAN'T BELIEVE IT," Marcy Duncan said. "I never thought he'd move back here."

"I know," Sheila Weaver chimed in. She shook her head, then drained the rest of her margarita. "It's…surreal."

That was one word for it, Eden thought, surveying the crowd of women assembled in her living room. However, were anyone to ask her, *nerve-racking* would be the description she'd use.

Kate—bless her wonderful, accommodating heart—had arrived early, the booze Eden had asked for in hand, and had relayed the scene to Eden without sparing any details.

According to Kate, Bennett had been shocked but apparently not angry. Frankly, Eden was surprised. She'd expected Bennett to be livid. He'd always had a notoriously short fuse and a temper worthy of his Wilder namesake and heritage. Even more baffling, he'd actually *thanked* Kate for letting him know about Artemis525.

It boggled the mind.

It had boggled Kate's, too. And though Eden knew her friend would never admit it, Bennett's character had just jumped a bit in her estimation. She hadn't said as much, of course—Kate was a notoriously fierce friend and had been crushed and outraged on Eden's behalf when Bennett had broken her heart—but Eden knew it all the same.

Rather than sit here all night and marvel over the disturbingly thrilling news that Bennett Wilder was back in town, Eden decided it was time to officially call the meeting to order. They had business to discuss, after all. She and Kate had talked it over and, in light of Bennett moving back to help his grandfather, they'd decided that renaming the site was the right thing to do. In fact, Kate had actually suggested it, which had made Eden feel better all the way around. If it had been simply her idea, she would have been second-guessing her motives. At any rate, now it was simply a matter of getting everyone else on board.

She cleared her throat. "Ladies?"

The buzz of conversation slowly fizzled out and expectant eyes turned her way.

"I think we've pretty much exhausted the Bennett's-back-in-town topic," she said, smiling when a couple of women protested. "Now what we have to decide…is what to do about the Web site," she finished, preparing for the backlash she knew was imminent.

Marcy arched a perfectly waxed blond brow. "What to do about the Web site? What do you mean?"

"You're not suggesting that we shut it down?" Sheila asked, clearly horrified. Though she was now happily married, Sheila was still an active member in the club. Once a Bennett casualty, always a Bennett casualty, Eden thought, though she knew Sheila was here more for the camaraderie than for the Bennett-bashing. As a new mother who ran a home-based marketing company, Sheila didn't have a lot of time for friends other than the online sort. She loved being a part of the club, though Eden had to wonder how it made her husband feel.

A chorus of disgruntled nos and gasps of outrage swiftly ensued.

"No," Eden quickly reassured them. "I, uh…I don't want to shut down the Web site." She paused. "But I do think we need to rename it."

She also thought at some point they'd need to restructure the content so that it no longer maligned Bennett's character, but she didn't think now was the time to address that particular tidbit. Not that it would be much of a change. Though Bennett had gotten them all together and the Web site had been initially about him, it wasn't anymore.

"I don't think we need to change a thing," Kelly Briscoe said, joining the conversation. She pulled an unconcerned shrug. "Just because he's back doesn't change anything." Her green gaze hardened. "He's still a womanizing, heartbreaking bastard."

And you're still a wee bit bitter, Eden thought with a mental whistle as she and Kate shared a significant look. They had expected resistance from Kelly. Unlike all of the other members of the club, who had for the most part forgiven Bennett or at the very least moved on, Kelly had not. Frankly, forgiveness of any sort didn't appear to be in Kelly's character.

Eden and Kate had even discussed the possibility of Kelly being Artemis525, but considering that Kelly had always been very vocal about her uncharitable feelings for Bennett, it seemed unlikely that she would assume another name just to post the disturbing messages. Generally if Kelly had something to say, she said it. Eden felt her lips twitch. Holding back didn't appear to have ever been an issue for her.

Eden scanned the room, gauging everyone's response to Kelly's remarks. A couple of people seemed to agree, a couple clearly opposed and a couple appeared to be on the fence. Hopefully she'd be able to sway them in her direction.

Eden shoved a lock of hair away from her face. "Look, in light of the fact that Bennett is moving back here permanently, I really think that we should give him a *small* break. He's going to have a hard enough—"

"He doesn't deserve one," Kelly insisted, setting her drink aside. "Personally I think that this could be a lot of fun. Instead of figuring out ways to cut Bennett some slack, I say we figure out a few ways to give him hell." She crossed her arms over her chest and looked around the room, trying to rally some support. "He certainly didn't mind putting us through it."

"Oh, for pity's sake," Kate snapped. "I'm the first one to say that he's a bastard, but it was years ago. It's water under the bridge."

"That's easy for you to say," Kelly countered. "You're the only one here who never got burned."

"That only means she was smarter than the rest of us," Eden replied, shooting Kelly a quelling look. She didn't like the way this was going at all. "Look, I'm not saying to give Bennett a full pardon—I'm not talking about changing the way we run the site. But it *was* years ago. And if he had any other choice than moving back here, we all know he would have taken it." She paused, letting that little detail absorb. "He's here to take care of an aging grandparent, which is going to be hard enough as it is."

"Particularly considering who that aging grandparent is," Sheila said with a significant chuckle. "Mom said things got pretty rowdy today before Grady left." Sheila's mother worked at Golden Gate, as well.

Kate's lips rolled into a droll smile. "Eva took the confiscated liquor into her office after Bennett drove away with Grady and didn't come out until her shift was over at five."

Marcy gasped. "Eva Kilgore got drunk?"

"I don't know about that," Kate said, eyes twinkling. "But let's just say she wasn't entirely steady on her feet when she came out. And she was smiling."

"Taking care of Grady isn't going to be easy," Marcy conceded, her brow furrowed thoughtfully.

"No, it's not," Kate agreed. "Aside from being a cantankerous, rowdy perpetual hemorrhoid, he's going to need more help than what I suspect Bennett is aware of. Frankly, I don't know whether Eva talked to him about it or not, but Grady probably needs a sitter." She looked at Eden. "Did he seem aware of that at all when you talked to him?"

Kelly's eyes widened and her accusing gaze swung to Eden. "You've talked to him? When did you talk to him?"

Eden's face heated and her insides twisted with mild dread. She'd hoped to avoid this conversation. "I pulled him over this afternoon."

A chorus of gleeful tell-all oohs sounded in the room. Several of the women shared significant smiles and shifted expectantly in their seats.

"We've been talking about Bennett for the past

hour and you're just now telling us this!" Marcy gaped at her. "Fess up!"

"Did you pull him over before or after he'd gotten Grady?" Sheila wanted to know.

"Was he speeding? Ooh, did you give him a ticket?"

"Before. Yes. And no."

Marcy blinked, seemingly confused. "What?"

Eden let go a small breath. "I pulled him over before he'd gone to pick up Grady. He was speeding…but I didn't give him a ticket. I gave him a warning."

Kelly's nostrils flared. "Then I think that's the only break he should get. If it'd been anybody else, you would have given them a ticket."

"You know better than that, Kelly," Sheila admonished with a reproachful look. "Eden pulled Nick over last week and she didn't give him a ticket." She glanced at Eden. "Thank you for that, by the way. Our insurance is high enough as it is. Another ticket and we'd probably get canceled."

She'd known that, which was exactly why she hadn't given Sheila's husband a ticket. Eden nodded. "No problem." As for why she didn't give Bennett a ticket, it would have smacked of sour grapes. *You dumped me like yesterday's garbage. So here, have a ticket.*

She didn't think so.

"How did he look?" Marcy asked, and from the

hopeful expression on her face Eden knew she wished that she'd report significant weight gain or a balding pate.

Neither of which described Bennett Wilder. More like…

Hot. Wicked. Perfect. Dangerous.

A rebellious thrill whipped through her middle, causing her belly to clench against a tide of sexual longing that made the Atlantic Ocean look like a kiddie pool. That wicked smile and those sleepy eyes materialized all too readily in her mind's eye, making her breath momentarily interrupt its normal rhythm. Longing rose like a charmed serpent beneath her breast, curling sinuously around neglected hot spots Bennett's mere presence had managed to inflame after three years without so much as a spark of heat.

With effort, Eden cleared her throat. "He looked the same." *Translation: just as gorgeous as ever.*

Marcy's face fell. "Oh."

"So," Kate said briskly. "Back to the Web site. Do we have any suggestions for a new name?"

"Yeah," Kelly said. "BennettWilderSucks.com."

Clearly nearing the end of her rope, Kate closed her eyes tightly and tossed back the last of her drink. "Let's put it to a vote, shall we? All in favor of renaming the site raise your hand."

Every hand but Kelly's went up.

Kate nodded. "Then that settles it, doesn't it?"

"Wait just a minute," Sheila said cautiously. "I

agree that we need to rename the site, but I also think that letting Bennett off the hook without so much as a slap on the wrist isn't right, either."

Truth be told—even caring about him as much as she did—it didn't feel right to Eden, either, but she supposed him seeing the site would have to be revenge enough.

"Sheila's right," Marcy spoke up. "Water under the bridge or not, Bennett's drive-through dating broke almost every heart in here. That deserves some sort of retribution."

A dry chuckle erupted from Sheila's throat. "Short of one of us breaking *his* heart, I don't see that happening."

Sheila's comment drew a knowing laugh from everyone but Kelly, who'd gone oddly still and was gazing curiously at Eden. "That's it," she said a little breathlessly.

"What's it?"

She stared unnervingly—significantly—at Eden. "One of us needs to break his heart."

A tremulous smile curled Eden's lips and a whirlwind of dread spun through her middle. Surely to God Kelly wasn't insinuating what Eden thought she was. She couldn't—

Seemingly catching on to Kelly's unspoken suggestion, all of the women in the room turned to look at her, as well, and an excited rumble of consent buzzed around her.

"You were always his favorite," Sheila said, nodding thoughtfully. "If anyone here could give Bennett a dose of his own medicine, then it's definitely you, Eden."

She sincerely doubted that. Furthermore, even if it were true, she had no intention of putting herself out there like that. Yes, she would agree that Bennett deserved a little brokenhearted retribution for his past mistakes, but she damned sure didn't intend to be the author of that misery. Were she to even attempt it, she grimly suspected she'd be the one who'd end up fractured and miserable.

Again.

Not no, but *hell* no.

She gave her head a small shake. "Er…I don't think so."

Kelly snorted with a knowing smirk. "I figured as much. You were all for starting the club and the Web site when Bennett wasn't here, but now that he's back you want to take them down and roll over and play dead." She threw her hands up in disgust. "Just what the hell are you afraid of?"

Of falling for him all over again, Eden thought.

Of believing in those old-soul eyes.

Of wanting him more than wanting her self-respect.

Of waiting for his kiss with bated breath.

Of jumping every time her phone rang.

Of feeling her heart leap every time a knock sounded at her door.

"I'm not afraid of anything," Eden lied, tilting her chin up defiantly because it was not in her nature to show fear of any sort.

"Then do it," Kelly challenged. "Do it for all of us."

"I—"

"Do it for all of us and you won't hear another peep out of me on renaming the site or plotting further revenge," Kelly told her.

"Come on, Eden," Marcy cajoled, gazing beseechingly at her. "It's just a little dose of his own medicine. It's not like we're asking for a pound of flesh."

Maybe not of his, but what about hers? Eden thought wildly, feeling the atmosphere in the room swiftly change. They were all looking at her as though she alone held the power to break Bennett's heart. Did she believe that they'd had something special? Even that he'd cared for her?

Yes, despite everything that had happened, she did.

But that didn't mean that she could do what they were asking. It was too much. She glanced at Kate, certain that her friend would come to her rescue.

Kate merely wore a thoughtful expression and shrugged.

Eden glared at her. Kate knew how hard it had been on her when Bennett had left town. Eden had been a shattered, miserable, ice-cream-eating wreck and had grieved for months. Kate couldn't possibly think this was truly a good idea, but she didn't seem inclined to voice an objection. Did she hate Bennett that badly? Eden wondered, surprised at her friend. Furthermore, the duplicity didn't sit right with her, regardless of what Bennett had done. Purposely setting out to hurt someone wasn't her style. Balancing the scales of justice from time to time? Yes. But this?

"I know it's a lot to ask, Eden," Sheila finally said. "But I can't tell you how happy it would make me to finally see Bennett get his." She hesitated. "A little humility would go a long way, don't you think? Especially if he's back in town for good."

She did. But she still didn't want to be the instrument of this plan. Unfortunately, Eden thought as she glanced from face to hopeful face staring at her, she didn't see any way to refuse without looking like the ultimate coward.

And that was unacceptable.

The theme music of the doomed running through her head, Eden finally nodded. "I'll try," she lied, crossing her fingers behind her back.

The Ex-Girlfriends' Club collectively whooped with joy. Or, every member with the exception of herself. She was too sick with dread and trepidation to celebrate.

7

BENNETT DROVE SLOWLY DOWN Eden's street and noted a line of cars snugged against the curb in front of a small steep-roofed church. Like most small Southern towns, Hell had always had a deeply religious presence, but attending church on Monday night was a little extreme even for them.

No doubt they were having a meeting of sorts, planning a fund-raiser for the mission fund or some other godly pursuit, possibly even praying for *him*, he thought, and the idea drew a reluctant chuckle. Let 'em, Bennett decided. He could use all the help he could get at the moment, particularly of the divine sort.

Bennett peered at the mailboxes, trying to discern which one of these houses belonged to Eden. He'd located her address using the same sorry dial-up Internet connection he'd used to scope out the Web site. His dread escalating right along with the agonizingly slow loading time, when the page had finally surfaced, Bennett had found himself alternately amused and nauseated.

The welcome page featured a rather large picture of himself, which had been altered to resemble a mug shot. Rather than holding an inmate number, the little sign he supposedly carried said Bastard. Phrases were pasted like warnings all over the page.

Caution: Avoid This Womanizing Asshole at All Costs!

Heartbreak Ahead!

Fast Talker, Faster Exit!

Player!

Guaranteed Misery!

And the mother of all insults: Premature Ejaculator!

While he wouldn't argue with the rest of them, *that* warning was a total fabrication. He hadn't lost control of his launch sequence since he was a teenager, dammit, and a young one at that. *Premature ejaculator, my ass,* Bennett thought now, irritated all over again.

In addition to the home page, Bennett had a page dedicated solely to him, named simply the Perpetrator. All of his vital statistics, as well as a lengthy essay enumerating his many faults, accompanied multiple pictures the women evidently had donated.

Another page featured the Victims, better known as the women he'd dated and subsequently hurt. Each one had a picture of the two of them together— some where he'd simply been Photoshopped into the scene—and her own personal Bennett story.

They accused him of "hit-and-run romance" and called themselves his casualties. Some were straight and to the point, chronicling their time together and how he eventually dumped them. Others were riddled with vitriol and expletives which called into question, most notably, the size of his brain in comparison with the size of his penis.

He liked to think both were significantly above average, dammit.

Naturally, Grady had peered over his shoulder and cackled. "I'd heard about that," his grandfather had told him. "You sure know how to piss the women off, boy, I'll give you that."

Exasperated, Bennett hadn't even bothered asking his grandfather why he hadn't relayed the information to him—anything that would have defeated Grady's purpose sure as hell wasn't going to get brought to Bennett's attention, that was for damned sure.

But the more Bennett had read, the more convinced he'd become that his apology to Eden was no longer anything he could put off. He'd known when he'd left town that he'd hurt her. He wasn't proud of the fact that he'd been too cowardly to say goodbye. But he truly hadn't realized the extent of the pain he'd caused her—and the other women— until he'd scrolled through the initial archives on the blog associated with the site.

Thankfully, Bennett had noted that the topic of conversation slowly turned away from him and onto other, more girlie things. Every once in a while, one of the members would go out on a bad date and make an offhand comment about how the guy had "pulled a Bennett," but otherwise things seemed to have moved into better territory.

Naturally, the posts from Artemis525 were a little disturbing, which was another reason he'd like to talk to Eden. It wasn't every day that one read about the possibility of having one's heart run over with a lawn mower or having his privates slashed off and crammed up an orifice he'd long ago deemed as "exit only."

The other ladies' rants and insults were the typical brokenhearted comments. Artemis525's rang with an unexpected, out-of-place—almost comical—menace that didn't jibe with the rest of the site. No wonder Kate had said Eden was concerned. He was mildly concerned, as well, inasmuch as he'd let a woman intimidate him, at any rate.

Which was very damned little, he thought with a grin.

Where on earth was her house? he wondered, backtracking around Arctic Circle once again. (The city of Hell had an interesting sense of humor, he'd give them that.) Bennett consulted the house numbers a second time and then did a double take when he realized that the little church he'd noticed had the same address he'd found for Eden online. Intrigued and bewildered, he pulled over and stared at it, certain that he had to be mistaken. "Well, I'll be damned," he murmured, stunned.

A church?

She'd been living in the apartment above her parents' garage the last time they'd been dating, and he knew she'd been anxious to move out—her mother, neurotic reigning queen of Hell, tended to smother her—but into a church?

He smiled and shook his head. Typical Eden, he thought. Why buy a little brick rancher when a church was so much more interesting? She'd always been interested in architecture, Bennett remembered. No doubt the arched lines, stained glass and cut stone had appealed to her. He scanned the line of cars in front of her house and felt another jolt of curiosity hit him.

Even more interesting…what were all those people doing there?

Bennett killed the engine, exited the car and pocketed his keys. No time like the present to find out, he decided, some grim sixth sense telling him that it probably had something to do with his unexpected return to Hell.

He let himself into a freestanding wrought-iron gate that wasn't attached to a fence, and admired the neat lawn and flower beds as he made it up the walk, noting the little touches that should have tipped him off to the fact that this building had been repurposed.

Hanging baskets bursting with blooms hung from the small front porch, and the typical American flag had been replaced with one featuring birdhouses and geraniums. A big tabby cat lolled on the porch, but bolted at him and hissed loudly the instant he put his foot on the first step.

Startled, he oomphed, swore and instinctively stepped back, then cursed himself for being cowed by a cat. He glared at it, then deliberately put his foot back on the step.

The cat hunkered low, into a ready crouch, and made an unearthly *loud* keening yowl that made the fine hairs on the back of Bennett's neck stand on end. Its amber eyes glowed eerily in the porch light and it continued to growl at him low in its throat.

Sweet mother of— What the hell was wrong with this cat? Bennett quickly backed up again. Not because he was afraid, of course—that would be too galling to bear, seeing as he was supposed to be a badass—but because he didn't think Eden would appreciate him hurting her cat, even in an act of blatant self-defense.

True to today's luck, someone chose that particular moment to open the door, and a group of women laughed and chatted amiably as they walked out onto the porch, unaware of his presence.

"God, this is going to be so good," one enthused. Marcy Duncan, if he remembered correctly.

"I know. I can't wait for Ben—" Sheila Weaver's

gaze suddenly landed on Bennett and she stopped short, her mouth hanging open in comical shock.

Marcy followed her stunned gaze and let out a little gasp of surprise. "Bennett," she said, smiling the sort of smile that made him instantly uncomfortable. It suggested she knew something important that he didn't.

"Evening, ladies," he replied, nodding as more women filed out onto the porch. He recognized all of them, of course. With the exception of Kate, he'd dated every damned one of them. So here was his Ex-Girlfriends' Club in the flesh, Bennett thought, resisting the urge to shift uncomfortably. He felt his cheeks burn, and thanked the darkness that hid it from them. Between the attack cat and the animosity rolling at him from the porch, Bennett had to admit he wasn't exactly feeling the love. That didn't keep him from appearing completely relaxed, though. He'd learned to master his emotions a long damned time ago.

"Well, well, well," Kelly Briscoe said with a brittle smile. She shared a conspiratorial look with the rest of her group. "Speak of the devil."

So he'd been right. They *had* been talking about him.

And if Kelly was in on the conversation, then he could only imagine the tone of that little chitchat. There were lots of things he'd regretted doing, but *doing* Kelly Briscoe was definitely in the top three.

She'd chased him for months—calling him, showing up at his apartment—and she'd always managed to mysteriously find him when he was out and about town. Having heard the "clingy" rumors about her, Bennett had managed to successfully avoid an entanglement. But after overhearing Kelly's sanctimonious father tell someone that he didn't have to worry about his daughter getting mixed up with Bennett Wilder because she had better sense, Bennett had amended his don't-fool-around-with-Kelly policy just long enough to get a dinner invitation so that he could see the look on her old man's face. Bennett grimaced.

It had almost been worth it—*almost* being the key word.

Kelly had latched on to him like a needy parasite, and he'd had one hell of a time shaking her off. Judging from the evil die-bastard-die look she was giving him now, she hadn't forgotten, much less forgiven him for it.

Eden pushed her way forward. "Bennett," she said. "I—I, er…wasn't expecting you."

That much was clear, he thought, offering her a pointed but droll smile. "You don't say? I'd wanted to talk to you, but—" he cast a meaningful glance at her entourage "—clearly this isn't a good time."

"Actually…" Kate piped up, starting deliberately down the front steps. She paused and petted the cat from hell, garnering an uncharacteristic purr from the feline. "This is an excellent time."

"Perfect," Sheila Weaver concurred with another oddly significant look. She followed Kate down the steps, and the rest of the group—all of them wearing interesting smiles that made him distinctly uneasy—filed past him until the only thing standing between him and Eden was her infernal cat.

Eden smiled a bit uncomfortably and gestured toward the animal. "I see you've met Cerberus."

Bennett felt a grin tug at his lips. "Cerberus, as in the three-headed dog that guards the gate to Hades?"

She nodded once. "That'd be the one."

He felt a smile tug at his lips. "Interesting name for a *cat* guarding a *church,* Eden."

Eyes twinkling with guarded humor, Eden bent and scooped up her kitty. "I actually got her before I moved here, but I do appreciate the irony." She nuzzled the cat, making Bennett momentarily jealous, and though it was probably only his imagination, he thought the cat looked a little smug. Eden hesitated, clearly torn. "Would you like to come in?"

Now that he was here, he wasn't exactly certain that he'd made the right choice. Ordinarily, he didn't second-guess himself, but Eden had always had a way of knocking him off his game. "Are you sure you don't mind? I should have called first, but—"

"It's fine," she said, not quite convincingly, but he'd take it. She turned, her long hair swishing over the small of her back, and gestured for him to follow her inside.

She'd changed out of her uniform and into a pair of khaki shorts and a white tank top. Both showcased a tight, curvy little body that instantly conjured ideas of naked flesh, of pert nipples and a weeping sex. Of long hair sliding over his chest and the sweet spot behind her ear, which had always smelled like spring rain.

Bennett had never been able to look at her without wanting her, but knowing just how far out of reach she was now seemed to have made her lethally appealing. His blood burned through his veins, pooling in his loins with a ferocity he'd only ever experienced with Eden. Because she was his first? he wondered, never quite far from that perfect memory, one of the few in his misbegotten life. Or simply because he'd never, despite his best intentions, been able to resist her?

In the end, what did it matter? He wanted her…and grimly suspected he always would.

He belatedly noticed that a silver toe ring winked from her bare foot and an interesting tattoo—one he couldn't quite discern from this distance—hovered above her right ankle. That was new, Bennett thought, equally impressed and turned on.

With an unhappy mixture of desire and unease dogging his every footstep, Bennett shoved his hands in his front jeans pockets and made the short trip over her threshold.

"Wow," he murmured, his gaze drawn upward to the vaulted ceiling. She'd left the original leaded-glass Gothic-style windows in place, and rather than dividing the rooms with walls that went all the way to the ceiling, she'd merely partitioned areas off with the standard eight-foot variety. It gave the house a sense of definition but left the fantastic architecture still viewable.

Eden gently deposited the cat onto a nearby armchair. "Behave," she admonished in a low voice. She turned to Bennett. "Thanks," she said softly. "It took a little while, but I finally got it how I wanted it."

"When did you move in here?"

"A couple of years ago. Things over the garage got too intense, so I bought the first thing I could find. I hadn't counted on it being a church, but—" she smiled and pulled a shrug "—it quickly became home."

And considering she was making the move away from pure evil—namely Giselle—moving into a holy site was probably prudent. Her mother's skin probably burned when she set foot in the yard.

"Hold on," Eden said, strolling toward the back of the house. "I'll get you something to drink."

Southern hospitality, Bennett thought, giving his head a small shake. He could be her mortal enemy—and probably on some level was—and yet she couldn't resist being a good hostess. Bennett murmured a thanks and wandered around her living room, appreciating her artwork, soaking in her atmosphere, and felt another wave of longing wash through him. She'd done several headstone and memorial rubbings of people she evidently admired and had them matted and framed. He read Dorothy Parker's and chuckled. *"'Excuse my dust'."*

Eden returned and handed him a beer. Their fingers brushed, igniting an electrical charge that caused her gaze to tangle startlingly with his. *Yes, I felt it,* Bennett silently answered.

Dammit.

"She was funny," she said, nodding toward the picture in a blatant attempt to break the tension. "Have you ever read anything of hers?"

Bennett felt a little odd accepting the alcohol in what used to be a church, but since the building hadn't caved in when he walked through the door, he took it nonetheless. "No, I can't say as I have."

"You should. She's hysterical."

Next to Dorothy Parker's he found Bette Davis's. *"'She did it the hard way.'"*

Eden cocked her head and released a rueful chuckle. "I think that can be said of most women."

"I would agree—" he cast a cautious look at the preening, haughty cat "—but I'm afraid you'll set that evil feline upon me."

"Cerberus isn't evil," she said, feigning insult. "She's merely protective. She might not be as loud as a dog, but she's every bit as loyal and vicious."

Bennett poked his tongue in his cheek. "I noticed that. When she was getting ready to attack me."

"You should be glad none of the other hellcats here tonight tried to attack you," she pointed out significantly, the corner of her ripe mouth tucking into an almost smile.

Bennett laughed, conceding the point. "There is that." He paused, sent her a hesitant look. "I'm equally lucky that you haven't yet, either."

Something unreadable flashed in those beautiful green eyes. "Don't get too comfortable," she warned. "I could still pounce without warning."

He sure as hell didn't doubt that. Though her temper had never been as violent as his own, Eden's fuse often varied in length, usually in direct correlation with the perceived injustice. Be it firecracker or nuclear bomb, you could always count on some form of explosion as a result of a wrong. He'd wronged her in the worst possible way—he'd broken her heart. At some point, Bennett knew she would detonate on him…and he deserved the blast.

Perversely, he looked forward to it. Anything would be better than this agonizing awkwardness. Like waiting for the other shoe to drop.

"So…I guess you're here about the Web site?" she asked, smoothly changing the subject.

His drink stalled halfway to his mouth and he studied her over the lip of the bottle. "In a manner of speaking."

"Have you seen it?"

Bennett nodded, his gaze tangling with hers. "I have," he admitted. "That's, uh…that's some impressive work. Was it all yours?"

Eden considered him for a moment, evidently unsure of what to make of his attitude about the site. No doubt she'd expected him to blow a gasket and go off on her about it—reasonable, considering that's what he would have done in the past—but other than being slightly irritated and mildly amused, he hadn't been able to muster any real anger over the site.

He'd deserved it.

Or most of it, at any rate.

"I did the majority of the work on the site, yes," Eden finally admitted, lifting her chin in that adorably belligerent way of hers. Her eyes twinkled with wicked humor. "What did you think of the mug shot?"

"That was a nice touch," he conceded. Bennett grimaced and took a pull from his beer. "Though I take exception to the 'premature ejaculator' warning."

Eden laughed, the first genuine chuckle he'd heard since he'd walked through her door, and he felt it move through him, break a bit of the tension hovering around them.

"*That* wasn't my work. Every member got to come up with their own warning for the home page." She paused thoughtfully, seemed to be mulling it over. "That was Kelly's, I believe."

Bennett snorted. That figured. Vindictive witch.

"You don't seem surprised." She hesitated, chewed the inside of her cheek and said, "You know, Bennett, every guy has an off night every once in a while. You shouldn't beat yourself up about it. I've heard that Kelly is pretty demanding in the bedroom, so if things went a little haywire—"

Bennett almost choked on his beer. His gaze swung to hers and, in the nanosecond before he could tell her that she, of all people, ought to know better, he discerned the hint of a smile hovering around her ripe mouth.

"Very cute," Bennett told her. "You know, I don't give a damn what you put on that site so long as it's accurate." He let his gaze drift slowly over her body, purposely reminding her of the truth. Stupid, he knew, because it made him want her all the more. But… "And *that's* not."

A low stuttering breath leaked out of Eden's lungs, and he had the privilege of watching those clear green eyes darken with remembered heat. Her lids drooped and her warm gaze dropped to his mouth. And lingered. She absently licked her lips, then her gaze tangled with his once more. In that instant he knew her mind had gone to the same place his had.

To a long-ago summer night three years ago.

Just like old times, they'd spent the day together, combing the back roads, looking for a secluded spot to make love. Every place in town had been exhausted, so they'd had to start widening their circle. Hell, he'd never been able to keep his hands off her.

Take now, for instance. Just breathing the same air as her right now made him feel more alive, more energized and more turned on than he'd been since the last time he'd seen her. It was as though she had the ability to flip a switch inside him. Everything became more colorful, clearer. Had there been other women? Of course. He was a man, wasn't he? But not in the past few months, because even unfulfilling sex got old.

And being with Eden had always been so…easy. Odd for him, when nothing else up until that point in his wretched life had been. They'd ridden out to Suicide Lane, a long, straight stretch of road that abruptly ended with a cliff. The combination of danger and the view—Hell, oddly picturesque from that vantage point as it glowed like a diamond cluster in a sea of inky blackness—had made it a particularly special spot for them.

Armed with blankets and pillows, Bennett had backed his truck up so that they could lie in the back and watch the stars. Eden had snuggled in next to him, her hair spilling over his shoulder, and a contentment and peace had stolen over him so completely that he'd found himself curiously unable to breathe.

She'd chosen that moment to tell him that she loved him—unwittingly sending him into a tailspin that would rattle him to the point that he left town. Then she'd pressed a kiss to his jaw—just the softest touch against his skin—and he'd…broken.

The determination, anger and resentment he'd insulated himself with had just fallen away…and then he'd fallen for her all over again.

Moonlight and sibilant sighs, a yard of pale blond hair sliding over his chest. Pearled pale pink nipples, soft belly and softer thighs. Her tight body balancing over his, riding him… His dick swelled and a burst of heat blanketed his loins, remembering. His own Lady Godiva, Bennett had thought at the time.

She blinked, breaking the spell.

"I'll, uh…I'll see what I can do about a correction," Eden told him, backing up a bit.

"I'd appreciate it," Bennett said, his voice curiously rusty. Shit, Bennett realized. He'd been crowding her. Leaning in, drawn to her as always.

A line of irritation emerged between her brows, then she cleared her throat and looked away, seemingly trying to gather her thoughts. "That's what we were meeting about tonight."

"The Web site?"

"Yes. Even though we're quite attached to the name," she said drolly, "we've decided to change it."

"What?" Bennett asked, feigning surprise. "BennettWilderSucks.com isn't working for you anymore? Too tame?"

Smiling, Eden shook her head. "No." Her gaze

caught his and she hesitated. "It's served its purpose," she said vaguely. "And in light of the circumstances which have brought you back to town, well…"

They'd decided to cut him some slack, Bennett realized, even though she didn't appear to be able to say it. He nodded, silently acknowledging that he understood. "Thanks," he managed, then shot her a look. "Besides, you girls are swapping so many recipes, ISuck.com doesn't really seem to fit anymore, if you ask me."

Eden paused, and once again those green eyes sparkled with reluctant humor. "You read every word, didn't you?"

He pulled a shrug. "I was curious."

"And you're not angry?"

Still stuck on that, was she? "Stunned? Yes. Outraged over blatant untruths regarding my performance in the bedroom, the size of my penis and the size of my brain? Yes," he confirmed. "But angry?" Bennett shook his head, took another drink of his beer. "Nah. I was a jerk." He shrugged. "You retaliated quite creatively, I'll admit. And I deserved it."

Eden's gaze darted to his, startled and cautious and just the tiniest bit…annoyed? Bennett thought, puzzled by her response.

"So you're changing the name of the site?" Bennett moved on. "Should I be worried?"

Eden blinked. "Er…no. Not unless you object to www.bitchingfromHell.com?"

Bennett felt his lips twitch. "Bitching from Hell, eh?"

She quirked a brow. "It has a certain cachet, don't you think?"

He grunted. "It beats the hell out of the one you had, that's for damned sure. Can I expect to see my mug shot removed from your home page anytime soon?"

Eden winced and gestured with a small space between her thumb and index finger. "Baby steps."

A bark of laughter burst from his throat, followed by a long sigh. "I guess changing the name of the site is progress enough for now." More than he'd hoped for, so he'd be better off to count his blessings.

"So...what did you think of Artemis525's posts?"

"That's part of the reason I came by," he told her, glad for the reminder. "Do you have any idea who she is?"

Eden shook her head. "None. I was hoping after you'd read the messages that you might be able to shed some light on the situation."

Bennett frowned. "It's odd, isn't it? How she just started posting?"

"It is," she agreed. "Have you dated anyone recently who might have stumbled across the Web site?"

Bennett shook his head. "No. I haven't had a lot of time for dating." And everyone else was just a substitute for her, so he'd developed a why-bother attitude. A thought struck and he frowned. "I thought Kate said that the two of you suspected a local girl?"

"Yeah, we do. It's a local ISP address."

"Then that would rule out anyone I might have dated since I moved away from Hell, right?"

Her brow wrinkled with belated recognition. "That's right." Eden set her beer on a nearby table. "Look, I don't know exactly what we're dealing with here—you read her posts so you know as much as I do—but you need to be careful and you need to report anything suspicious."

He frowned skeptically. "Oh, I don't think—"

"Bennett, this could be serious," Eden insisted. "You can't afford to take it lightly."

Was she genuinely worried about him or was this merely professional advice? Bennett wondered, hoping for the former.

"Look," Eden continued doggedly. "I'll let you know when she posts to the board if you promise to let me know if anything out of the ordinary happens."

A bark of laughter broke up in Bennett's throat. "Out of the ordinary? In Hell?"

Eden chewed the inside of her cheek. "You know what I mean." She shot him an endearingly fierce look, tempered with the smallest smile. It was so reminiscent of how she used to be that it made his breath momentarily catch in his throat. "Promise me," she insisted.

Secretly pleased with her concern on his behalf—and, pathetic jerk that he was, he'd take it regardless of her motives—Bennett finally nodded. "Fine," he told her. "But I'm sure that it's nothing."

Eden didn't argue but merely nodded, and an uncomfortable silence yawned between them, one he knew he should fill with the apology he'd come here to deliver.

He looked away, passed a hand over his face then found her gaze. "Look, Eden. I wanted you to know how so—"

"Don't, Bennett," Eden interrupted, clearly anticipating what he'd planned to say. She squeezed her eyes shut for the briefest of seconds, as though stopping him was painful for her. "I know what you're going to say—or try to say—and I'd…I'd rather you didn't. I'm not ready."

To forgive him, she meant, Bennett realized, feeling his midsection deflate with a sucker punch of regret. If she wasn't ready after three years, then she probably never would be. For whatever reason, the thought of never getting her absolution was almost worse than knowing she could never be his, that he'd blown it one too many times with her. That's what he'd wanted, Bennett realized. What he needed more than anything—her forgiveness. Up until this very instant he hadn't understood just how important her pardon was.

Clearly he wasn't going to get it right now, but

next to taking care of Grady, that had just become priority one.

"I, uh…I should probably get going," he told her, feeling himself inexplicably lean into her space once more. He released a long sigh, fisted his hands at his sides to keep from reaching out and touching her. "God only knows what Grady has gotten into while I was gone."

More than likely the alcohol, Bennett thought. His grandfather was a little too fond of the hard stuff, but telling the old man not to indulge was like trying to pry a chocolate bar away from a scream-ing toddler.

Ultimately not worth the effort and mess.

Eden tucked her hair behind her ear—an endear-ingly nervous habit he recognized from their times together—and padded behind him to the door. "Did Eva mention Grady needing a sitter to you?"

Surprised, Bennett looked down at her and frowned. "A sitter? No."

She grimaced. "Oh."

"Why?"

"Well…Kate feels like he probably needs one."

Bennett knew that Grady was going to require a good bit of time, if not care, but a sitter? He blinked, taken aback. Had it really come to that? "Even with me there?"

"You'll be working outside a lot, right?"

Bennett nodded. He'd already thought of that,

which was why he'd planned to install an intercom system between the house and the barn. He told her as much.

"That certainly ought to help."

"I'm planning on hiring a full-time house-keeper," Bennett said thoughtfully. "Someone to come in and cook and clean. So he won't be alone much, even when I'm working."

"Then maybe she could pull double duty," Eden suggested.

Bennett snorted. "*Covert* double duty. If Grady thought for a minute I was hiring someone—a sitter, of all things—to take care of him…all hell would break loose."

Eden chuckled softly, conceding the point. "Then what he doesn't know won't hurt him."

Bennett smiled down at her. "And there's that." He paused and fought the natural—almost over-whelming—urge to lower his head and kiss her. She was so close, a mere nod of his head away, and seemed to be getting closer by the second. He could see every fleck of lighter green in those amazingly clear eyes, the spattering of freckles over her nose and the hint of moisture lurking on her bottom lip.

Fire burned through his veins and his dick strained hard against his zipper—an inevitable oc-currence around her. The delicate slope of her cheek begged for his touch and her ripe mouth beckoned like heaven for a damned man.

And that was why he ultimately pulled away.

He couldn't have her now any more than he could have had her three years ago. He'd ruined himself for her, had—in a bitter twist of irony, thanks to her mother's stay-away-from-my-daughter mandate— literally *made* himself unworthy of her. In thumbing his nose at the town—at everyone who'd ever thought he wasn't good enough—he'd ultimately thumbed his nose at their future.

And Eden Rutherford deserved better.

Bennett swallowed a sigh, deflated by the reminder. Unable to help himself, he bent and pressed a lingering kiss against her forehead, then he squeezed his eyes tightly shut and pulled away while he still could. His feet felt rooted to the spot and it took every ounce of effort he possessed to make them move. "Good night, Eden."

Confusion—and commiserating regret, may-be?—momentarily cluttered her gaze, but she blinked it away before he could be sure.

"G-good night, Ben," she replied softly.

8

"GOOD MORNING, DARLING," Aunt Devi trilled from her yoga mat. "There's a muffin on the table for you. I'll only be a minute."

Used to interrupting her aunt in one way or another, Eden shuffled tiredly into the airy kitchen and found a homemade cranberry-date muffin waiting on the battered oak table for her, along with a tall glass of fruit tea.

She'd been asking her aunt for the recipe for years, but to no avail. Devi insisted on "willing" it to her, just as her own aunt had done for her. The Darlaston women were an odd bunch, with lots of curious customs passed down from generation to generation. The willing of the recipe was only the beginning, Eden thought, grimacing as she bit into her muffin.

She had another tradition swiftly approaching that she wasn't quite prepared for.

Patting the back of her neck with the corner of a towel and looking much younger than her sixty-plus years, her aunt strolled into the kitchen. She wore a purple sports bra and matching shorts, and her handmade earrings dangled from her ears. "You have bags under your eyes, dear. Didn't sleep well?" she asked with a mysterious smile.

Fitfully, Eden thought, shooting her aunt a guarded look. Then again, a visit from Bennett Wilder would do that to a girl. Less than an hour in his company and she could feel herself swaying toward him, could feel her resistance withering under the heat of the attraction. And that sweet kiss to her forehead... Jeez, God, was he trying to kill her? Did he know how hard it had been not to reciprocate the gesture? How difficult it had been not to wrap her arms around his waist and rest in his strength?

What little sleep she'd gotten had been plagued with dreams of the two of them—in the back of his old truck, specifically that night parked at the end of Suicide Lane. Quite honestly, the chemistry between them had always hovered around fever pitch, but something about that night had simply been...*uniquely intense.*

Intense enough that she'd tipped her hand and told him that she loved him.

A gesture by which he'd evidently been so touched he'd left the next morning without so much as a thank-you-for-the-great-sex—but it had been pretty damned special to her, at any rate. So much so, in fact, that it seemed to have completely ruined her for another guy. There'd been a flicker of attraction between her and another man on the force, but a flicker hardly measured up when she'd been used to a blaze.

Eden murmured a noncommittal sound in answer to her aunt's question, then took a sip of her tea. She moaned with pleasure, thankful to have something to be happy about. "You know, it's quite terrible of you to hold this recipe hostage from me until you die."

"Piffle," her aunt teased. "It gives you something to look forward to."

Eden felt her eyes widen. "Your death?"

"No," Devi said. She poured herself a glass of tea and added an orange wedge. "Getting the recipe. It'll be a bright spot in an otherwise dreary time. Trust me, I know."

Well, she couldn't argue with that, could she? And no doubt it would be a terrible, terrible time. Devi was like the mother she'd never had. Warm and witty, always waiting with a kind word or a laugh. Eden didn't know what she would have done without her.

"Furthermore, if I give you the recipe, you'll stop coming to see me." She made a moue of displeasure and sighed dramatically. "And then I'll be old and alone and unloved."

Eden snorted, jarred away from her dismal musings. "You are so full of *shit*."

Devi might be old*er,* but she was still the most vibrant, effervescent and unique person Eden had ever known. She had dozens of interests—yoga being her newest thing—and even more friends. Old, alone and unloved, Eden thought again, sliding her aunt a glance. *Ha!*

Devi tsked. "Such cheek." Her bright blue eyes twinkled. "Your mother would be horrified."

Too true, Eden knew, inclining her head. Giselle Rutherford couldn't be any less like her sister. Sadly, Eden's mother put the *P* in *propriety,* the *B* in *boring* and the *S* in *snob* and, more often than not, the *B* in *bitch.* When she was growing up, Eden had often fantasized that she was actually Devi's daughter but for dramatic, romantic reasons she would never know or comprehend, she'd been given to Giselle to raise in her stead.

In all truth, she favored Devi more in temperament and appearance than she did her mother, but seeing as she wouldn't trade her father for anything in the world, Eden always felt bad for dreaming of a different parent. Did she love her mother? Of course.

Eden frowned. But she couldn't say that she particularly liked her very much.

Constantly critical—of everything, not just her—Giselle rarely found favor with anything. Eden never came away from an encounter with her without feeling as if she'd never quite hit the mark or measure up to Giselle's standards. How her father stood it, Eden couldn't imagine. They say love is blind, but in this case Eden thought it had to be deaf and mute, as well. Uncharitable? Yes. But sadly accurate.

To make matters worse, Giselle had always been horribly jealous of her older sister, so having a daughter who was more like her rival than herself had to be hard.

It sure as hell had been hard on Eden.

"Speaking of the Dragon…" Devi said, using the nickname she'd long ago given her baby sister. "This came in the mail this morning." She handed Eden a small parchment invitation. "Funny," her aunt mused, shooting her a veiled look. "I wasn't aware that you'd chosen your new name yet."

Eden felt the muffin do a donut in her stomach. "What?" she asked, horrified, as she skimmed the invitation. "Oh, no," Eden murmured, anger, irritation and dread hurtling through her middle. "No, no, no!" She bolted up from her chair, and her wild-eyed gaze clung to Devi's. "How could she do this? I told her I hadn't found a name yet! That I wasn't ready! I have until the end of the year, dammit. Why now? Jeez, God," Eden said through partially gritted teeth. "Why does she always do this?"

Devi pulled a delicate shrug. "Your mother's motives are her own, dear. I have no idea why she's forcing your hand."

Eden scanned the invitation once more and felt her blood boil and an angry tick start near her left eye. "She's booked the venue, selected a caterer.

Everything," Eden said disgustedly. "Without asking me," she all but growled. "And it's *my* naming ceremony."

Per tradition, the Darlaston women didn't give their children middle names. It had all started with Eden's great-great-great-grandmother, who at twenty-eight had decided she didn't like the name her mother had shackled her with and decided to change her middle name to one she actually liked. When her children were born, she purposely only gave them one name so that when the time was right they could choose one for themselves.

Of all the Darlaston traditions, Eden had to admit that she appreciated this one the most. A name was special, a definition of character. How many people, given the opportunity, would change their name? Would have chosen something different from what their parents had given them? She liked the idea of selecting her own middle name…she just hadn't found one yet.

Since Grandmother Anastasia—her chosen name, as she'd been born Lois—hadn't known until she was twenty-eight what sort of name she wanted, the family had adopted that deadline for future generations. Sometimes they figured it out early, sometimes it was last minute, but the family invariably hosted a blowout party for whoever was choosing her new name.

Eden had imagined something lively, fun and

casual hosted at the Ice Water Bar and Grill. What her mother clearly had planned was more like a debutante ball.

Her grim gaze swung to Devi's once more. "I'm not doing this."

"Jamison Hall isn't cheap. The deposit alone had to be hefty."

"Then she'll lose it," Eden said, unconcerned. "This is *my* name and *my* naming ceremony. It's about me, not her." A futile growl rose in her throat.

"She won't be happy."

Eden's lips formed a humorless smile. "Then she should have asked first."

Devi considered her for a moment, then nodded, seemingly impressed. "Good girl." She paused. "Now about this name…still no thoughts?"

Eden released a small sigh and shook her head. "I've been looking, I really have." Frowning thoughtfully, she mashed a muffin crumb onto her thumb and ate it. "As much as I hate to admit it, I can't seem to find anything I like better for myself than the name Mom chose for me."

And it was the truth. She liked her name. It was classy without being pretentious. Of Hebrew origin, the name meant "pleasure." She liked to think that she was a pleasure to know, to work with and to be around. It suited her.

"Well, you've still got time," Devi told her. "I didn't find my name until the midnight hour, as well."

Eden grinned. "Yes, but you found the perfect name for yourself. You *are* a goddess."

Devi grimaced. "I certainly wasn't an Ester."

Eden chuckled and shook her head. "No, you weren't."

"I understand you had a visitor last night," Devi said, eyeing her shrewdly.

Uh-oh. "I had several. Which one in particular are you referring to?" She knew, of course. What blew her freakin' mind, though, was how did *she* know? Her aunt had always been the go-to girl when it came to town gossip, but this was pretty damned fresh. How the hell had she found out about it already? And, better still, who else knew?

"Bennett," her aunt said, shooting her a pointed look. "Was he invited or did he just drop by?"

Eden leaned against the counter. "He dropped by."

"After he visited the Web site, I imagine," Devi said, chuckling. "Well?"

"Well what?" Eden hedged.

Devi heaved a patient sigh. "What did he want?"

With the exception of *her,* Eden wasn't altogether sure. Nevertheless, she would be lying if she said that knowing that Bennett still wanted her hadn't been like an ointment to her still-smarting pride.

The months after he'd left had been sheer hell, and she'd spent the majority of that time thinking that he'd merely had his fill of her again, something everyone had warned her about.

But she and Bennett *had* enjoyed a *meltingly* wonderful sex life. The tops of her thighs burned just thinking about it. It had been wild and frantic, desperate and thrilling. The smallest thing—a simple sleepy-eyed look from him—would make her so hot that her sex would actually throb in anticipation. No matter where they were or what they were doing, finding a place to stop and make love had never been a problem.

The bathroom at the Ice Water Bar and Grill? Check.

The fitting room at Mona's Dry Goods? Check.

The coat closet at city hall? Check.

Not to mention all the times they'd merely climbed into the cab of his truck or ducked into a handy restroom. With Bennett…Eden simply couldn't explain it. The desire—the drive—had been more powerful than the fear of getting caught and of, ultimately, getting hurt.

Even knowing what she knew now—that he'd dump her *again* without so much as goodbye, much less an explanation—she'd do it all over again. She didn't regret it. Couldn't, when she suspected that the kind of passion they'd shared was of the rarest sort. It was the kind that made men fight unwinnable battles, divided families and forever changed the landscape of a soul. She swallowed.

It had certainly changed hers.

He'd also wanted to apologize. And because she

was terrified of accepting that apology, she'd put him off. She needed the distance. Knew herself well enough to realize that the minute she accepted his regret, she'd lose some emotional ground she wasn't altogether certain she'd be able to make up. A pitiful defense, she'd admit, but she had to work with what she had. A sincere apology from him would undermine her ability to keep her guard in place.

"Eden?"

She blinked, pulled from her reverie. "Sorry," she mumbled. "I was woolgathering."

Devi's eyes twinkled with sympathetic humor. "I've gathered my share of wool over a man before, dear."

Eden knew that was true. Her aunt had carried on a secretly thrilling but painful affair with a man whose identity to this day was still unknown. Eden had tried many times to wheedle it out of Devi, but to no avail. Eden didn't know who owned her aunt's heart, but it had prevented Devi from ever marrying or having children of her own. If her aunt had any regrets, though, she'd never shared them with her.

"You never told me why Bennett dropped by," Devi reminded her, evidently determined not to let the subject drop.

Eden let go a small breath and gave her aunt the least complicated answer. "He'd read the Web site—Artemis525's posts, specifically—and wanted to know if I had any idea who she was."

Devi was the second person Eden had gone to with her concerns the minute Artemis525 had started posting to the board.

"Do you?"

"No," Eden admitted. "Not a clue."

Concern weaved a grave line on her aunt's brow. "Do you think he might be in danger?"

"He could be," Eden admitted. "The messages are disturbing and they're coming from a local ISP address, which means whoever she is, she's from around here."

Devi frowned again. "What are you going to do?"

Eden shrugged helplessly. "I don't know. At this point there's really nothing we can do. She's just posting messages—posted another one late last night, as a matter of fact—but she has only threatened him." Eden took another sip of her tea. "And Bennett's got enough to worry about without throwing a psycho into the mix."

"What do you mean?"

"Grady," Eden said significantly.

Her aunt's eyes widened in understanding. "Oh."

She relayed Kate's concern that Grady might need a sitter. "Bennett's planning on hiring someone to come in and cook and clean. He's hoping that'll help."

Devi's gaze turned curiously speculative. "He's looking for a housekeeper, you say?"

Eden paused. "Yes. Why?"

Her aunt sat up a little straighter and an odd

gleam had entered her usually impassive gaze. "I might be interested."

Eden choked on a surprised squeak. "You?"

"Don't look so shocked, dear," her aunt admonished, drawing herself up. "I enjoy domestic tasks and I happen to be a pretty fine cook."

"I know that," Eden said, still a bit shocked. "I just wouldn't have thought that you'd be interested in something so…"

"So homey?" her aunt finished for her. "I realize that it's not as exciting as some of my other occupations, but it can't be that hard."

Eden snorted. At various times during her life her aunt had been a tour guide, a flight attendant, a flying trapeze instructor and a personal assistant to Robert Kennedy. She was a master gardener, had developed her own line of cosmetics and was currently into jewelry making. The idea that she wanted to apply for the position of Bennett's *housekeeper* was…incomprehensible.

Furthermore, we were talking about Grady Wilder here. Lovable, of course, but ornery and very difficult to get along with. She couldn't see her aunt putting up with his crap, that was for sure.

Eden shook her head. "I'm sure that you'd be a shoo-in and I doubt if he's had time to hire anyone yet. You should call him if you're seriously interested."

Devi nodded decisively. "I am."

All righty then. Eden rinsed her glass and set it

in the sink. "I should get going," she told her aunt, letting go a droll sigh. "I don't think the taxpayers would appreciate me spending my whole shift hanging out with you."

"You earn your keep," Devi told her. She smiled. "Getting Jeb to give up those crosses is a job."

Eden chuckled, then hugged her aunt, once again grateful for her support. "That's one word for it. Thanks for the muffin and the company."

"Anytime, dear." She frowned. "Now what's the new name of the site again? Bitching from Hell?"

"That's it. It'll be a few days before I've got it transferred, so the original domain name will work for a little while longer." Eden made her way to the door.

"So…what did the Ex-Girlfriends' Club have to say about Bennett being back in town?"

"You mean apart from the general oh-my-God-I-can't-believe-he's-back buzz?" Eden grimaced. "They elected me to reel him back in and break his heart."

Devi's eyes widened and she gasped. "What?"

Eden gave her head a hesitant shake. "No worries," she said. "I'm not doing it. I lied and told them I'd try, but…" Eden looked away, then found Devi's gaze once more. "Self-preservation, you know. And a general sense of it's just not right. Setting out to purposely hurt someone? Even someone who might deserve it?" Eden paused and lifted her shoulders in a helpless shrug. "I'm all for justice, Aunt Devi, you know that. But it's just not me. I'm not up for that job."

Devi offered a sympathetic smile. "So what are you going to do?"

"I'll tell them that he wasn't interested." Which wasn't a total lie. He hadn't even been interested enough before to tell her goodbye.

Devi winced. "But didn't he arrive at your house before all the girls left?"

Where the hell was she getting her information? Eden wondered again. She frowned at her aunt. "He did."

"Will they believe you, then, when he's already singled you out?"

Eden had thought of that. Still… "I'll make them believe it."

Her aunt gave her a skeptical smile. "Okay, dear. Let me know if you need any help."

Eden couldn't imagine what exactly her aunt could do to help her out of this situation, but she appreciated the sentiment all the same.

For whatever reason, she got the distinct feeling she was going to need all the help she could get.

9

"WHAT THE HELL IS THIS?" Grady demanded.

Summoning patience from a higher source, Bennett set the sugar-free syrup on the table and took his seat. "It's an omelet."

Grady glared at the offending eggs. "It's white."

"That's because it's an egg-white omelet." Same conversation, different menu, different day. And it was only day two. Bennett smothered a long-suffering sigh.

He *had* to hire a housekeeper.

Grady jabbed a fork at the eggs in apparent disgust. "Did I ask you to leave the yolks out of my omelet?"

"You didn't ask me for an omelet at all. You asked for breakfast. I made it. The polite thing to do would be to eat it without complaint and say thank-you when you are done."

"I would have done that if you'd left the yolks in my omelet and given me some syrup with some sugar in it. What the hell is wrong with you?" Grady scowled. "Why are you trying to make me eat this healthy crap?"

"So that you'll live longer," Bennett said, baring his teeth in a smile. "Because you are such a joy to be around."

"Smart-ass," his grandfather groused. He poured enough salt over the eggs to make every blood vessel in his body constrict, then shot Bennett a dirty look and rebelliously doused them with hot sauce. "How'd you sleep?" he asked gruffly.

Like shit, Bennett thought. Between thinking about Eden—a problem he'd tried to amend by keeping so busy he fell exhausted into bed every night—and his miserable mattress, he hadn't caught more than a couple of winks. He didn't remember his mattress being quite so lumpy, but it had been a long time since he'd slept in this old house, so he didn't know whether his memory was faulty or he'd simply been spoiled with the comfy pillow-top variety he'd gotten used to in Savannah.

Though he'd paid the neighbors to maintain the grounds and periodically check on the house, the old two-story still had a neglected feel about it when they'd arrived home the night before last. Bennett had spent the majority of his time yesterday getting things put away and organized, not to mention he'd spent several hours in town buying groceries and stocking staples.

True to form, everywhere he'd gone people had stared and whispered behind his back. He'd barely resisted the childish urge to turn around and scream, "Boo!" but had ultimately gone about his business.

To his great surprise, however, many people were quite friendly and had welcomed him back like a long-lost relative. Funny how his success had changed their perspective. The big question, of course, was did he plan to open a store here in Hell? Not at the moment, Bennett had told them, but a quick drive through the downtown area showed surprisingly busy foot traffic.

Nothing on the Savannah scale, but for Hell pretty impressive. If he could find the right space, he might reconsider the idea of putting in a second store. The tourist trade seemed to be booming, after all, and the renovations and whatnot on the farm certainly weren't going to come cheap.

Other than splurging for his car and some high-end tools, thanks to his grandfather's respect-every-dollar advice, Bennett had managed his sudden wealth with a cool head. He'd invested well, put money back for a house. He hadn't expected it to be his grandfather's, but... Bennett mentally shrugged. He was doing all right for himself.

Thankfully the bulk of his things would arrive today—including his bed—so despite dealing with his cantankerous if lovable grandparent, things were moving along nicely. He looked forward to setting up shop and getting back to work. Inspired by Eden's Gothic windows, he'd sketched an idea for a new chair last night and was eager to get started. He missed the feel of the wood beneath his hands, the drag of the blade against the grain. The raw smell of oak and oil.

His world.

Doris, his shop manager, had hit him on his cell this morning and told him that he'd had six new orders come in via their Internet site over the past couple of days. Two were from repeat clients, but the other four were new business, which was always nice to hear. Overall, things were shaping up quite nicely. Now if he could just get some good help in here—someone his grandfather wouldn't run off— he'd be in excellent shape.

As if on cue, a knock sounded at the back door.

Grady looked up, startled. "You expecting some-body?"

He'd expected Ryan this morning, but the arrival of last night's storm and ensuing rain had changed those plans. Ryan had called this morning to re-schedule. A small setback delivered by Mother Nature, but it couldn't be helped.

Bennett frowned, pushed away from the table and stood. "The movers, but they aren't scheduled to be here before three." In addition to the rain, which he hoped would move out by then, he had a lot of rearranging, clearing out and cleaning to do, so he'd purposely asked for a later arrival time. In-trigued, he made his way to the back door.

"Good morning, Bennett," Devi Darlaston said brightly. Wearing big earrings and a bigger smile, the older woman stood on the back porch, an enormous picnic basket in one hand and a small wrapped package in the other. She'd leaned her dripping umbrella against the wall next to the door.

Bennett heard his grandfather's fork fall to his plate. "Devi?" he choked.

"Er…good morning, Ms. Darlaston," Bennett said, surprised to find Eden's aunt on his doorstep. "What a nice surprise." It was a surprise, at any rate. Whether or not it would end up being nice remained to be seen.

"Oh, thank you, Bennett," she said, strolling into his kitchen. "Call me Devi, please. Ms. Darlaston makes me feel so old. Oh, and I found this on your step." She handed the little package to him.

Intrigued, Bennett took the gift from her and set it aside.

Looking oddly surprised, Grady still gaped but had recovered enough to mind his manners by standing. "Devi," he said suspiciously, his brows furrowing into a bushy line. "What brings you here?"

"Eden mentioned that you were looking for a cook and a housekeeper. I'm here to apply for the job, if it hasn't been filled already, of course."

Grady's mouth fell open again. "You? But—" His gaze dropped to the basket she'd set on the table. He gestured toward it. "What have you got there?"

"Oh, a little something I whipped up this morning." She opened the lid and started unloading various dishes. "A nice breakfast casserole, maple link sausage, bacon and ham, biscuits and jelly, hash browns and the like."

Grady unceremoniously dumped his original breakfast into the trash and loaded his plate with Devi's admittedly better heart-attack-waiting-to-happen variety. Bennett had to admit that it smelled heavenly.

"So Eden told you I was looking for someone?" Bennett asked, watching his grandfather enthusiastically attack his new breakfast.

"She did," Devi told him. "She comes by most mornings and shares a glass of tea with me." She paused as though just remembering something important. "Which reminds me…" She pulled a lidded jug out of the basket. "I brought along a little fruit tea, as well. Would you like a glass, Bennett?"

Bennett had heard Eden rave about the tea in the past. If memory served, this was the recipe she was supposed to inherit from her aunt. A ghoulish custom, if you asked him, but he wasn't so put off by it that he didn't want to try the tea. He pulled a few glasses down from the cabinet and waited while Devi poured.

He took one sip and hummed with pleasure. His gaze swung to hers. "You'll make this for us if you come to work here?"

Devi smiled. "Of course."

"Then you're hired," Bennett said without preamble.

"What?" Grady bleated. "But—"

Devi arched a quelling brow. "Are you unhappy with my breakfast?" she asked.

His grandfather lowered his gaze sheepishly. "No. But—"

"Do you doubt that I can keep a clean house?"

"Of course not, but—"

She smiled sweetly. "Then what legitimate objection can you possibly have?"

Bennett watched the exchange between Eden's aunt and his grandfather with speculative curiosity. He was picking up on an interesting undercurrent between the two of them but had no idea what it could possibly be about.

Devi pulled an apron out of her basket and tied it into place. "I came prepared to start. We can work out terms later." She paused and cast him an almost sly look. "Though I do have a question. As I mentioned, Eden often visits me for breakfast. Since I'm going to be making that meal here, do you have any objection to her coming over from time to time?"

Eden? Coming here? On a regular basis? How the hell was he supposed to be noble and keep his hands to himself if she was showing up here for breakfast? How was he supposed to resist her if he saw her regularly? Bennett cleared his throat. "Not at all."

"Excellent." She looked around the kitchen. "We'll let Grady finish up breakfast, then you can tell me what the most pressing items on my to-do list will be."

She'd picked a wonderful day to show up, Bennett thought, because everything on his to-do list was pressing.

As though she were familiar with the layout of the kitchen, Devi began tidying up. She handed him the package she'd brought in earlier. "Don't you want to see what this is?" She smiled. "Looks like you've got a secret admirer."

Bennett chuckled darkly. He doubted that, but took the little box anyway and carefully opened it. A small plastic box lay inside with a card attached to the top. Intrigued, he picked it up.

Welcome home, Bennett. Here's what your heart is going to look like when I get finished with it. I'm hunting and the time is drawing near.

A fist of dread bolted through him. *Oh, shit.* Though she hadn't signed the card, Bennett knew who this particular little gift was from. He pulled the plastic container from the box and carefully opened the lid. He drew back, revolted.

"What you got there?" Grady wanted to know.

Devi, too, turned around. She frowned. "Is something wrong?"

"Er…where did you say you found this?"

"On the back step. It was just sitting there." Seemingly concerned, she moved forward and peered into the container. "Oh, my," she said, her gaze flying to his.

Sufficiently fed, Grady's curiosity finally propelled him to his feet. "What?" he wanted to know. He scowled at the contents and looked at Bennett. "Someone gave you chicken livers?"

"Is that what this is?" Bennett asked.

"Yes," Grady grunted. "You ought to recognize them. Used them enough when we were fishing with 'em."

Ah, Bennett thought, remembering. And not fondly. While Grady had been a real outdoorsman, Bennett had not. He hadn't cared for hunting or fishing or any of the other grisly pursuits of wildlife that involved him maiming or killing another animal. Don't get him wrong—he liked a steak as much as the next man. But he preferred to buy it from a deli case in the back of the grocery store. No doubt he would have made a rotten caveman.

Devi worried her lower lip. "Do you think it's from her?"

So Eden had shared that with her aunt, as well? Bennett thought, handing over the card. "It has to be."

"Her? Her who?" Grady asked, sniffing the livers. "These still smell all right. Think you could cook them for dinner?" he asked Devi.

Devi scowled. "No. And they're from your grandson's stalker, for heaven's sake. You think I'm gonna cook something a stalker has left behind?"

Grady looked as if he'd been beaned over the head with a frying pan. He glanced at Bennett, clearly torn between being afraid on his grandson's behalf and cackling. And if it had been anyone else's grandson, Bennett knew Grady would have crowed with merriment. His face burned.

Grady cleared his throat of a chuckle. "You've g-got a stalker?"

Bennett flushed even more. Oh, for God's sake… "I don't know that I'd call her a stalker, per se, but—"

"She's a stalker," Devi said forcefully. "Did you read the card? She wants to turn your heart into chicken livers." She nodded determinedly. "You have to call the police."

Bennett instinctively balked. "I—"

"Bennett, this is serious," Devi said gravely, clearly outraged that he didn't want to alert the authorities to the threat.

But, dammit, it was *galling*. All the way around.

In the first place, he was a man, and therefore supposed to be able to take care of himself.

In the second place, her motivation in and of itself was humiliating. He'd been a womanizing bastard who'd broken her heart?

Thirdly, on the off chance that the Web site wasn't common knowledge, he'd have to disclose that. More embarrassment.

And what about keeping things low-key? Blending in? He could hardly do that if he became the subject of a full-fledged investigation. Bennett's face heated, his head began to throb and the back of his neck tightened with tension.

Devi drew herself up. "Bennett, if you don't call them, then I will. This is serious. It's no longer a harmless threat hanging out in cyberspace. She's arrived at your back door."

True, he knew. Still…

"Call Eden, then," Devi suggested, clearly running out of patience. "I have her cell number and she's on duty this morning."

Promise me, she'd said. And he had. Rather than breaking another one he'd made to her, he should probably try to start keeping them. Bennett heaved a long, miserable sigh. "Fine," he told them. "I'll call her."

Grady peered into the container once more. "You're sure we can't use these?" he asked Devi.

Eden's aunt heaved a disgusted sigh. "They're evidence, you moron. Of course not."

Curiously, Grady didn't take exception to the insult. Which was odd, when he would have rounded on anyone else. Bennett paused and frowned at the two of them. Clearly there was more here than met the eye. Unfortunately—or fortunately, depending on how one wanted to look at it—he didn't have time to mull it over. He had to call Eden and let her know about his chicken-liver lunatic.

Perversely—because he had evidently lost his mind—he found himself oddly delighted that he had an excuse. *Happy* to have a stalker if it meant seeing Eden again.

How screwed up was that?

As screwed up as she'd always made him.

10

THE LAST PLACE EDEN EXPECTED to find herself this morning was standing in Bennett's old farmhouse kitchen, inspecting a carton of chicken livers.

Then again, stranger things had happened.

Looking distinctly uncomfortable but adorably sexy all the same, Bennett grimaced and leaned against the counter. "I feel like an idiot."

Grady grunted. "Why do you feel like an idiot? It's not your fault that you've inherited my good looks and considerable sex appeal. I've been known to drive the women crazy myself," he said, smugly rubbing his hand over his grizzled jaw. "'Course, I've never made a *stalker* out of one, but—" he slapped Bennett on the back "—then again, I've never had your talent for pissin 'em off the way that you do." His twinkling gaze darted to Eden. "When are you planning on updating that Web site of yours with some new information? I could use a good laugh."

Devi snorted and rolled her eyes. "You *are* a good laugh."

Eden felt her lips twitch. "It'll be in the newsletter."

Bennett's eyes widened and he choked on a drink of her aunt's fruit tea. "Newsletter?" he wheezed. "There's a newsletter, too?"

Though it was tough, she managed to flatten a smile. Bless his heart, despite everything, she couldn't help but feel a little sorry for him. True to form, Hell's grapevine had been producing juicy blow-by-blow tidbits since the instant he moved back into town.

Though she hadn't seen him since the night before last, Eden knew that Bennett had bought batteries, tinned biscuits—practically blasphemous in the South—and Fruity Flakes. Odd that she should find his choice of breakfast cereal endearing. And yet she did, Eden thought, her lips twisting into a small smile.

In addition to his trip to the grocery store, he'd visited the local hardware outlet, as well. It was common knowledge that Bennett had hired Ryan Mothershed to handle the renovations and that Sue-Ellen Fieldstone, president of the Hell chamber of commerce, had cornered him personally regarding his putting a shop in the downtown area. A notorious flirt, no doubt Sue-Ellen would have liked to have made the visit private, as well, but according to various eyewitnesses, Bennett had calmly but firmly let her know that he wasn't interested.

A new leaf, the gossips had speculated—or had he simply become more selective? Eden had no idea, and though she would love to add a she-didn't-care to that, too, she found herself miserably unable to make the declaration. She'd been heartened—and relieved, dammit, if she were honest with herself—that Bennett had rebuked Sue-Ellen's advances.

Bennett moving back was hard enough. Bennett moving back and immediately dating someone would be practically unbearable.

And of course, if the Ex-Girlfriends' Club had their way, *she'd* be dating him again. She mentally winced at the reminder.

Eden had called Kate from her cell phone on the way out here to let her know that Artemis525 had left a calling card on Bennett's back porch. Aside from being appropriately unnerved, Kate had taken the opportunity to remind Eden of her *promise*—now that was a stretch—to the Ex-Girlfriends' Club.

Surprisingly, Kate had been quite in favor of her being the one to pay back Bennett for the heartbreak he'd inflicted on their friends, and the more Eden argued the point, the more tenacious Kate had become. Quite frankly, it annoyed the hell out of Eden, but rather than looking like a coward—or showing the slightest bit of weakness where Bennett was concerned—Eden had simply gone along with the ruse.

Was she really going to try to break Bennett's heart? No. Even knowing he deserved it, she couldn't bring herself to attempt it. She had her own heart to think about, dammit. Granted, she hadn't exactly done a bang-up job of it in the past....

Eden glanced at the open container of chicken livers and the accompanying note, then inwardly grimaced. But thanks to Artemis525 she'd at least be able to make a pretense of doing what they'd asked of her. Until they figured out who was behind Bennett's threats, she had a feeling she and Hell's favorite bad boy were going to be spending a lot more time together. Her gaze slid to him and her belly gave an expected but unwelcome little jolt.

Of the sexual-longing variety.

Which was hardly surprising when she'd never, at any point in recent memory, found him anything short of *magnetic*. The moment she'd looked into those dark-as-sin, sleepy-looking eyes again a couple days ago, it was as though her flatlined libido had been hit with a defibrillator. Even now she could feel the sexual energy—his singularly potent pull—coursing through her veins, lingering in long-neglected hot spots. The tips of her breasts, the tops of her thighs, the heart of her sex. Eden released a slow, shaky breath.

But how was she supposed to find him anything short of irresistible when he looked like that? Dressed in worn jeans—*really* worn, not the trendy designer faux ones which were currently on the market, but honest-to-goodness lived-in, washed-until-there-was-no-strength-left-in-the-fabric-denim, which hung low on his narrow hips and draped every lean, muscled inch of his body from the waist down.

Most notably his ass, which had always been better than perfect.

He'd paired the jeans with a white designer T-shirt—equally flattering as it molded to wide shoulders and a muscled chest, one that had been honed with actual work instead of just a workout. A leather cord with a silver Chinese charm hung from around his neck, and a pricey-looking watch—TAG Heuer, maybe?—encircled his wrist. He looked casually successful and completely comfortable in his own skin, which was a powerful turn-on in and of itself.

It was also new, Eden thought, shooting him a covert look. Bennett had always been a bit wary and restless, on guard and very rarely at ease. She paused, watching him closely. Clearly his move to Savannah had given him more than a fabulous career and a boost in income—there'd been an internal change, as well, one she was secretly attracted to.

Oh, hell. Who was she kidding? Was there anything about Bennett—aside from his penchant for breaking her heart—that she didn't like or find attractive?

No, dammit.

Equally a turn-on was the fact that he still wanted

her—at least physically, at any rate—as well. Despite the multiple helpings of shit on his plate, Eden couldn't help but notice—and feel—those compellingly dark eyes sliding over her body the instant he opened the door. He'd swallowed, inexplicably licked his lips, and that too-hot gaze had lingered over her mouth to the point that she'd felt herself actually leaning toward him, drawn like a magnet to his wickedly sensual mouth.

Wickedly talented, too, Eden thought, releasing a stuttering breath as images of what he'd done to her in the past with that mouth flitted rapid-fire through her mind. Kissing her…everywhere.

And, good Lord, could he ever kiss.

There was nothing quite so flawless, so romantic, so amazing as the anticipation of the perfect kiss…and then having it surpass your expectations.

Ben Wilder was a premier kisser.

He'd mastered the delicate balance between wet and dry, the artful brilliance in the draw and drag between hungry lips. He didn't just kiss—he made love with his mouth. Every silky warm slide of his tongue mimicked the most intimate act between a man and a woman, and by the time the natural order of a seduction had segued into the next act, Eden had generally been on the verge of climax before he'd even gotten her naked.

After he'd sampled the back of her neck—a particularly sensitive spot for her—the angle of her jaw, then nibbled on her breasts and feasted between her thighs, she would be a pulsing hormone of make-me-come mush.

Like now, Eden thought, resisting the pressing urge to fan herself. Or disappear with her magician to the nearest bedroom. God help her, she was doomed. She had to stop thinking like this. She was her own worst enemy. Her own freaking down—

"Are you all right, dear?"

Eden blinked, belatedly realizing that the concerned question had come from her aunt and had been in reference to her. "Er…yeah," she murmured, feeling her cheeks pinken.

Devi hummed under her breath. "You seemed a million miles away."

Would that it were true, Eden thought, releasing a small breath. Her gaze darted to Bennett, who was looking at her with a slightly smug expression. No doubt the wretch knew exactly where her million-miles-away expression had taken her.

Right back into his bed.

Eden cleared her throat, fervently wishing that he couldn't read her so damned easily. "So you found it on the back step?"

"Your aunt did," Bennett told her, looking uncomfortable once more. "She insisted that I call you."

Eden felt her lips twitch. "So you've said." Several times, in fact, she thought, feeling the slightest twinge of pity for his embarrassment. The idea of needing help of any sort—particularly because of a woman—had to be utterly galling for him.

"And this was all you found? Just the note and the container?"

Bennett nodded.

"Well…" Eden sighed as she carefully sacked up the evidence. "It's a standard tub of chicken livers, marked with a Hefty Heifer sticker, which means—"

"That it's from the local grocery store," Bennett finished. "I'd noticed that."

Devi put a hand to her throat. "You mean these were bought in town?"

Eden nodded at her aunt. "Exactly."

Her worried gaze darted to Bennett. "Then she's a Hellion. It could even be someone we know."

Considering Hell was a relatively small burg, in all probability it *was* someone they knew. Eden grimaced, considered the note once more. "She's bent on breaking your heart, isn't she?"

Bennett's lips slid into a humorlessly droll smile. "Funny. I got the impression she wanted to hack my heart from my chest and slash it to pieces."

Grady, showing the first bit of concern, shot a wary look at Bennett. "Jeez, son," he murmured quietly. "What did you do to this girl?"

Bennett's uneasy gaze tangled with hers. What he'd probably done hung unspoken between them, the proverbial elephant in the room. The silence swelled around them until he finally managed a halfhearted laugh and pulled a shrug. "I'm not sure, Gramps. Maybe she'll tell me before she kills me."

"Oh, now, we'll hear none of that," Devi admonished, patting Bennett on the arm. "You've done the right thing by calling Eden. She'll protect you, won't you, dear?" Her aunt smiled expectantly, as though she'd asked Eden to pass the salt as opposed to opening a vein.

Eden felt her face freeze and her heart rate soar. Her gaze darted to Bennett's. Knowing humor danced in those dark brown eyes and he forcibly flattened his lips to keep from smiling. Her? Protect Bennett? Eden thought, swallowing.

Er…then just who the hell was going to protect her from *him?*

"DO YOU THINK I NEED PROTECTING, Eden?" Bennett asked, enjoying her discomfort entirely too much. The idea of him needing a protector was laughable enough without Eden's horror-stricken look of dumbfounded misery. Her aunt had quite neatly— and quite purposely, if Bennett had his guess—just put her on the spot. She couldn't say no without coming off as a)an unconcerned bitch or b) not doing her job. Both of which were unacceptable to her.

It was a neat little box, he reflected speculatively, not unlike the one the chicken livers had arrived in.

And she'd been served right up at his door, too. Interesting…

A better man might not entertain ways to use the situation to his advantage, but over the past couple of days Bennett had spent more than the usual amount of time thinking about Eden—a feat he wouldn't have thought possible, as he usually thought about her all the time anyway. A couple of days ago he'd made apologizing to her—earning her trust again—priority one.

Did he deserve her now any more than he ever had? No. Giselle Rutherford had made sure of that. But this wasn't about what he might or might not deserve—it was about Eden. And Eden deserved to know that he was genuinely sorry for hurting her. She didn't want to hear it, of course—she'd cut him off cold the night before last for even trying. But because she was fair-minded and just and noble, she *needed* to hear it. And because he was a greedy, ungrateful wretch, he needed her absolution. Staying in Hell wouldn't seem like such a miserable thing if he had that.

The problem with trying to properly apologize to her—to let her know how terrible he felt about the way things had happened between them—was time. Merely running into her here and there wasn't going to do it. He needed more than a casual conversation with her and, short of showing up at her house uninvited again, he didn't see her planning on sharing a lot of the same air as him.

Sad that, Bennett thought, when breathing the same air as her was all that used to make him feel whole. He swallowed, pushing the memories back. All it did was make him think about how badly he'd screwed up, how wrong he'd been, and made him wish for a life that was completely lost to him now.

Eden cleared her throat. "I don't know that you need protecting," she said. "But I do think that you're going to have to be really careful."

"What about a restraining order?" Grady asked.

Eden shrugged helplessly. "Against who? We don't know who she is yet."

Grady frowned, stymied. "Well, it's probably one of those women who hang out around your site," he said. "Wouldn't that be the best place to start looking?"

Eden hesitated. "I've thought of that, Grady… and it just doesn't fit."

His eyes widened. "What do you mean it doesn't fit? Those women hate him," he said, his voice climbing.

"She is posting there, dear," her aunt kindly pointed out. "It's where she made her first appearance. Shouldn't you investigate everyone?"

"I've been picking around a little since she first started posting and I really don't think that it's anyone associated with the club."

Intrigued, Bennett cocked a brow. "Why not?"

Eden expelled a breath and shot him a cautious smile. "Because the women who frequent the site have never attempted to hide their identities or their, er, negative feelings for you."

Bennett snorted. Negative feelings, hell—they hated his guts. "You're right," he said. "Calling me a bastard is hardly sugarcoating it, is it?"

Eden's lips twitched slightly and she looked away. "Well," she said, "the point is, no member of the club has anything to hide. Whoever this is, she's someone who is using the site and the club's existence to further her own agenda and muddy the waters." She paused. "At least that's what I think."

Eden was right. He'd seen the archives and trolled the message board himself. Eden posted as herself, Kate and the lot of them, as well. Artemis525 was the only person who seemed to have anything to hide.

In addition, the timing seemed weird to him. His stalker had started posting the day after he and Grady had finalized his plans to move back to Hell. Because he'd wanted to keep gossip to a minimum—Bennett smothered a bark of dry laughter—he'd asked Grady to keep it under his hat. Eva had been too terrified that he'd change his mind about taking Grady off her hands to do anything but what he'd asked.

In short, aside from Grady and Eva, no one knew that he'd made arrangements to move back to Hell. Yet, for whatever reason, he got the distinct impression that Artemis525 did. He shared his opinion with Eden.

"I definitely don't think it's a coincidence," Eden told him. "No one other than Eva and Grady knew you were moving back?"

Bennett shook his head. "I wanted to keep things low-key."

Reluctant humor twinkled in those clear green eyes. "What? Turning over a new leaf?" she quipped.

Bennett grimaced, smiled and shot her a look. "More like the whole tree."

A soft chuckle bubbled out of her, and that genuine laugh moved through him, warming him. "What about Ryan?" Eden asked, moving on. "Would he have told anyone?"

Bennett paused, thinking back. He knew he'd asked Ryan to keep quiet, but more importantly, he hadn't contacted Ryan about the renovations until a week or more after Artemis525 started posting. He shared that with Eden.

"It's possible that Ryan said something about my moving back—he would have told his wife, I'm sure, as well as his crew—but the time line is still off. She'd already started posting before Ryan had gotten the information."

"I understand the significance of Artemis," Devi said thoughtfully. "But not the 525."

Eden inclined her head and shared a look of understanding with her aunt. "I know. I don't get it, either."

Bennett felt his brow wrinkle. "I don't get any of it. What are you two talking about?"

"The name she's chosen. In Greek mythology, Artemis was the goddess of the hunt." Eden paused and her hesitant gaze caught and held his. "In this case, I think you're the hunted."

Fabulous, Bennett thought, suddenly more than irritated. He was being hunted—*stalked*—by some unknown women for some unknown reason, being made a fool of and ultimately undermining what was already a stressful situation. Moving back to Hell was hard enough. Moving back and dealing with this unpleasant garbage—a direct reminder for himself and the town of his past sins—was even worse.

"I wonder if the 525 is a date," Devi said cautiously. "You know, like May twenty-fifth?"

Eden went unnaturally still and her gaze darted to her aunt's, then to Bennett's. "I'll bet she's right," Eden said, her voice oddly quiet with the realization.

"May twenty-fifth? But that's just—"

"Assuming that she knew you were moving back, I think that's exactly what it is. Like Artemis, it's part of a clue." Eden quickly reviewed the note again. "Yes," she said more forcefully, the adrenaline of figuring out the clue making her voice climb. "Look." She held the letter up for Bennett to see. "She refers to the hunt here. See? The 525 has to refer to a date."

"The twenty-fifth?" Grady said. "But that's just a few days away."

Four, Bennett realized. A week to the day since he'd moved back.

"Oh, my," Devi said, her eyes rounded with worry. "What do we do?"

Eden released a heavy breath. "Well, for starters, I need to get back to the station and talk to the chief. He'll need to—"

"No," Bennett said flatly.

Eden blinked. "What?"

True to his usual form, he was about to piss each and every one of them off—Eden most of all—but…*no*. He wasn't going to do this, allow this crazy woman to make a circus out of his life, make him a laughingstock. This was not how he intended to start over again in Hell. He was trying to repair his reputation, and the last damned thing he intended to do was publicize the fact that his previous whoring ways had landed him a psycho stalker. Bennett's head began to throb once more.

No, no, no.

He forced a smile, a calm he in no way felt, and made a valiant effort to keep his voice level. "I don't want you to tell the chief. I don't want you to tell anybody."

Eden shook her head. "Bennett, I can't—"

"That's why I called you on your cell phone. This isn't an official call, right?"

She hesitated. "Well, no. But—"

"No buts," Bennett interrupted her. "Seriously, Eden. I don't want anyone to know about this. I can handle it myself."

"Horseshit," Grady interjected. "You cannot handle this yourself. You're in over your head." He gestured to Eden. "Let her do her job."

Bennett closed his eyes, drawing patience from an almost dry well. "She can do her job…just off the record." He paused and his gaze met her wary one. "Can you do that, Eden? Will you?"

He didn't need her help—not really—he just wanted a reason to be with her, to make her forgive him. Probably manipulating her like this wasn't the right path, but at the moment it was the only one he could see. He couldn't apologize if she wouldn't let him near her, could he? And he had to apologize. He had to make things as right between them as he could. Naturally, the swiftest way to earn her forgiveness was to seduce it right out of her. But he had to try and do things the right way this time.

Eden froze. She opened her mouth, then snapped it shut again, seemingly unsure of what to do.

"Please," Bennett added, his gaze searching hers. "This is too much. Can you imagine the field day Hell will have with this? If this gets out, I don't have a prayer of starting over here." A bitter laugh broke up in his throat and he passed a hand over his face. "Not that I had much of one to start with, but…"

"Eden," her aunt implored softly on his behalf.

A beat slid into five, then ten. Then Eden, having considered him until he felt as if she'd probed right into his head, finally cleared her throat. "That's what you want here?" she asked, her voice curiously rusty. "A new start?"

Bennett nodded, surprised at how true those words were. He watched her chew her bottom lip and felt an arrow of heat land directly in his groin, silently cursing his reaction.

"Then I'll help you."

11

WELL, IT WAS OFFICIAL, EDEN thought as she made her way down to the Ice Water Bar and Grill to meet Bennett.

She'd lost her mind.

Offering to help Bennett—off the record, no less, which could potentially get her fired—couldn't indicate anything otherwise. She had to have had a mental break, some sort of psychotic episode—*something*—to have let those words come out of her mouth.

Then I'll help you.

Never mind the fact that she was supposed to be looking out for herself, protecting her own damaged heart. That spending any amount of time with him was dangerous to the point of stupidity because she'd already learned—twice, dammit—that she couldn't resist him.

Furthermore, being with him only gave him more opportunities to apologize, and the instant he did that, Eden knew what little bit of anger and hurt she'd managed to hold on to would no longer provide the armor she needed. She'd weaken, and when that happened, she was emotionally doomed.

Oh, hell, who was she kidding? She was doomed the instant he drove back into town. Every time she saw him, every time she looked into those dark-assin eyes, every time he inadvertently-on-purpose touched her—and that sweet, reverent kiss on her forehead, Eden thought, remembering the bittersweet pleasure of it and how desperately she wanted it to have been more….

Did she need to help Bennett? No. If she had a brain in her head, she would run so far in the opposite direction the hounds of hell couldn't catch her.

Unfortunately she'd glimpsed Bennett's underbelly—his most potent vulnerability—and saying no simply hadn't been an option. Bennett Wilder, badass extraordinaire, accomplished artisan, womanizer and all around heartbreaker, after all this time and for all his faults, still wanted the one thing Hell had always withheld from him—acceptance.

The minute Eden had realized that—that starting over was *that* important to him—she hadn't been able to tell him no.

Was he embarrassed by having a stalker? Certainly. But more than anything, she suspected that he was more terrified of the "field day" Hell would have with his predicament than of Artemis525 herself. Which was sad, not to mention a little misguided.

And the hardheaded fool *needed* to be afraid of

her—that's what was so annoying, Eden thought. He was so afraid of what everyone thought that he didn't have sense enough to be wary of a true physical threat.

Hell, she'd waltzed right up to his back door, bold as brass, and left that disturbing package and note. She was no longer just posting sick little messages onto their board—she was truly going after him. And if Devi was right—and Eden firmly believed that she was—then Artcmis525 planned to make her ultimate coup de grâce in just four short days.

To that end, Bennett had suggested that they get together and hammer out a plan. Rather than inviting him over to her house, Eden had decided that meeting him in public would a) hopefully keep her from tumbling right back into bed with him, b) further the illusion that she was doing what the Ex-Girlfriends' Club had asked of her and c) help pave the way for his reentry into Hell society. She was a public servant, after all, and the mayor's daughter. Bennett didn't necessarily need her stamp of approval, but being seen with her couldn't hurt his reputation.

Her lips twisted with bitter humor. In fact, were anyone's reputation in danger of a little tarnish, it was hers. After all, it was public knowledge that he'd dumped her twice—a fact her mother had taken particular glee in pointing out when Eden had contacted her about the premature invitations to her naming ceremony.

Surely to God you've got better sense than to get mixed up with that boy again, she'd said, injecting just enough disgust into her voice to set Eden's teeth on edge. *And for heaven's sake, take that juvenile Web site down. It's bad enough everyone in town knows you've been mixed up with a Wilder, much less splashing it all over the Internet. It's low-class. It's beneath you, Eden.*

Actually—like everything else from paper plates to costume jewelry—it was beneath her mother, but not her. Rather than argue with Giselle about Bennett, Eden had taken the opportunity to let her mother know that she'd canceled each and every one of the arrangements that had been made on her behalf for the naming ceremony.

She'd also taken out an apologetic ad in the paper and retracted the invitation. She'd neglected to tell her mother that, but rather kept it like a little present for herself. Her mother invariably started her day with a cup of imported designer coffee and a copy of the *Hell Times.* She could just imagine the look on Giselle's recently lifted face when she saw what Eden had done. She'd be mortified, which was the purpose, of course. After all, Eden had been equally humiliated and infuriated that her mother had attempted to hijack her naming ceremony.

Unfortunately, if she didn't want Giselle to make another go at it, Eden knew the time had come to plan it herself. She intended to talk to Mickey—

owner of Hell's infamous watering hole—about hosting the event for her at the end of the month. Had she found a name yet? No. But hopefully her self-imposed deadline would go a long way toward helping her make a selection.

Eden nudged her SUV up to the curb in front of Ice Water and released a tiny breath of apprehension, all she would allow herself. Yes, she was treading on shaky ground by meeting Bennett, but so long as she kept her footing and didn't wind up on her back, she'd be fine. She grabbed her purse and made her way inside, thankful for the cool blast of air that met her the instant she opened the heavy oak doors. A round of "Hey, Eden" welcomed her, causing a smile to play over her lips.

Dark paneling, eerie red lighting and shallow bowls of dry ice emanating foggy waves replicated Mickey's version of hell. Little fabric pitchforks dangled from the backs of the waitresses' uniforms and each one wore a pair of sparkly red devil horns on her head. Tourists loved the place for the decor, but the locals came for the food, most notably the hot wings. Eden found a table near the back and ordered a plate, along with a beer. She'd just lifted the bottle to her lips when she spotted Bennett weaving his way toward her.

It was a good thing she had something handy to quench her thirst, because he looked so damned hot that he fit right in with the theme of the restaurant. In fact, had he left a charred path in his wake, she wouldn't have been the least bit surprised. Heads turned, forks stalled at open mouths and the sound momentarily receded as he made his way to her booth.

Once again the epitome of the hip urban professional, Bennett had paired jeans with a black T-shirt—which upon further inspection revealed the phrase *I solemnly swear that I am up to no good*— trendy leather jewelry and equally hip leather sandals. Eden had never seen a guy successfully wear the shoes, but true to form, he pulled it off with masculine panache which set him apart from every other man in the room.

As always, he was effortlessly sexy, exuding a magnetic sort of charm that made the fine hairs on her arms stand on end, and made her belly clench with desperate longing she knew from experience only he could assuage. Oh, sweet mercy, how she wanted him.

He slid in across from her and smiled, though it didn't quite reach his eyes. "Are they still staring?"

Eden casually peered around him. "Some of them are, but most have lost interest."

Bennett swore hotly. "God, I'll never get used to it."

A twinge of pity pricked her heart. "The novelty will wear off soon."

"That's what I keep telling myself," he told her, wincing significantly as though he wasn't altogether convinced that it would ever happen.

"The more you get out, the quicker it'll pass. It's just because you've been gone so long."

"It's just because they're waiting for me to screw up again."

That, too, Eden silently concurred, but managed a reassuring smile all the same. "Then don't give them anything."

His dark gaze found hers, curiously making the breath in her lungs thin. "I'm trying, Eden," he said, an unmistakable sincerity ringing in his voice that affected her far more than it should. "That's why I've asked for your help."

And in that instant she was reminded once again why she'd offered it. He really wanted to make a go of things here, to be the stand-up guy his grandfather was counting on.

Eden cleared her throat. "What is it exactly that you want me to do?"

Bennett smiled, and a bit of humor twinkled in those dark, mysterious eyes. "That's simple enough. I want you to protect me."

Back to that, were they? The infernal wretch. She could just kill Devi. Eden snorted and rolled her eyes. "You're so full of crap."

He blinked innocently, though they both knew it was just an act. "What? You're the one who said I should be taking this more seriously. So I am. I want you to protect me."

No, he was just looking for an excuse to keep her

around so that he could apologize to her…among other things. She didn't know exactly how she figured into his turning-over-the-whole-tree approach, but she knew he wanted her absolution. He wanted to do things right this time—hadn't she just realized how important that was to him?—and by doing that, he needed to correct some old wrongs. No doubt he needed to put a check mark by her name. But for Eden's own self-preservation, she didn't need to let him do it.

She had her own heart to look after, dammit, and she had to be smarter about him this time. As much as it galled her to admit it, her mother was right. Bennett had made a fool of her twice, had hurt her more deeply than she ever imagined a person could feel pain. She wasn't up for that again, and only a moron with some sort of emotional death wish would allow it to happen for a third time.

Absolutely not.

She *had* to stay strong. She *had* to resist him.

Anything less was simply begging for more heartache, and she'd had enough of that to last her a lifetime.

Did she want Bennett to get his new start? Certainly. Despite everything they'd been through together, she wanted him to be happy. But aside from helping him out with his stalker, Bennett was on his own.

It was only four days, Eden told herself. She

could handle anything for four days, right? She looked across the table and felt her belly flutter with dangerous longing. She helplessly let her gaze trace the woefully familiar landscape of his face—dark, compelling eyes, sinfully carnal mouth and that smooth patch of ultrasoft skin just above his cheek and to the left of his eye—and mentally whimpered.

Four days. Four agonizing, miserable tempting days with the one and only man she'd ever loved and had never been able to resist.

God help her.

PREDICTABLY, SHE'D SEEN RIGHT through him, Bennett thought, studying Eden from behind the lip of his beer. Though he knew he should be more concerned than he was regarding Artemis525—of being hunted—Bennett found himself more worried about Eden bailing despite the true evidence of the threat.

Yes, she'd agreed to help him this morning, but that had been before she'd really had a chance to rethink her position. She'd been put on the spot and backed into a corner—his lips quirked—and if there was one thing a person could count on when Eden Rutherford was backed into a corner, it was that she'd come out fighting.

In what manner remained to be seen, but Bennett knew better than to trust that she would simply do as he asked. She was notoriously stubborn—not to mention sneaky when the need arose—and would cater to her own agenda, regardless of the consequences.

His gaze lingered over the sweet curve of her jaw, the smooth line of her cheek and that delectably plump bottom lip. God, he'd missed her, Bennett thought, swallowing past a sudden tightness in his throat. Had there ever been a girl he'd cared about more? Did he even have to ask?

No.

Because Eden had always simply done it for him. She was warm and witty, charming and opinionated. She was loyal and fair and moody and interesting.

She was *good,* Bennett realized with a start of warm insight. Would that she could share a little of that with him, he thought, grimacing. God knows, were anyone asked to use one adjective to describe him, *good* definitely wasn't going to be at the top of their list. He mentally snorted and his gaze slid to Eden once more. What would she say? he wondered. After all, other than Grady's, hers was the only opinion that had ever truly mattered. Did he want to belong in Hell? To be painted with his own brush and not that of his parents? Certainly. But in the end, Eden was the only person who mattered.

Fuck it, Bennett thought. He'd just ask her. "If you had to use one adjective to describe me…what would it be?" An abrupt subject change, but it wasn't as if the conversation police were going to swoop in and arrest him.

She blinked, seemingly startled. "What?"

"If you had to use one adjective to describe me, what would it be?"

She studied him cautiously. "I'm not sure—"

"Oh, for pity's sake, Eden, it's not a test," Bennett told her, shifting in his seat. "I'm just curious." He took a pull from his beer. "And don't sugarcoat it. Be honest."

Eden cocked her head in silent bewilderment, then considered him for a moment. A slow smile dawned across her lips and lit her gaze, making her eyes sparkle like fresh dew on new grass. "Well, it goes without saying that you're hot."

Bennett chuckled, flattered, the shallowest part of him inwardly preening with masculine pride. He'd asked for honest, hadn't he? "Thank you," he told her, his gaze on hers. "But I was actually thinking more along the lines of a character trait."

"A character trait?"

He nodded. "Yes, a good one, if I might make a request."

She made a moue of chagrin. "I thought you wanted honest."

"Smart-ass," Bennett murmured, laughing softly.

The corner of her mouth tucked into an adorable smile, Eden paused once more, seemed to be probing into his brain again, excavating his soul as she studied him. Finally she let go a small breath. "If I had to choose one word to describe you…it would be—" she squinted thoughtfully "—*talented.*"

Now that certainly wasn't what he'd expected. "Talented?"

"Yes," she said, sighing softly. "Not what you were looking for, eh?"

Bennett shot her a smile. "Well, it beats the hell out of *bastard.*"

Eden chuckled. "There is that." She paused. "Seriously, though, you are very talented. I've always thought that about you, and it's nice to see that you've been able to put that talent to work for you, that you're sharing it with others."

Bennett chewed his bottom lip. "And it doesn't hurt that it's lucrative. But thanks," he said, nodding, warmed by her compliment. Sure, she hadn't said that he was honest or loyal or noble—none of the traditional traits women usually appreciated in a man—but the one she'd chosen did suit him perfectly, and it was the one that meant the most to him.

"I don't know where that question came from, but turnabout's fair play. What about me? If you had to use one adjective to describe me, what would it be?"

Looking more relaxed in his company than she'd been thus far, Eden leaned against the back of the booth and regarded him with expectant amusement. Clearly the alcohol was having a positive effect, Bennett thought, his lips twitching.

"Well, it goes without saying that you're hot,"

he told her, boomeranging the compliment right back at her.

Eden grinned and nodded, evidently pleased. "Thank you. But I was looking for something a little more…substantial—a character trait, specifically."

Bennett poked his tongue in his cheek, enjoying this conversation with her more and more. He'd missed this, too, Bennett realized. Physically, there was no question that his body had practically gone into withdrawal. But this…fun conversation, relaxing with her. This had been absent from his life for too damned long.

He could tell her that she was good, and while she would undoubtedly appreciate it, Bennett knew it sounded too easy, too trite, so he improvised with a trait he knew she would appreciate. His gaze caught hers and held. "You're fair."

Eden paused, seemingly absorbing the implication of his assessment, then finally nodded, evidently pleased. "Thank you," she said. "I like to think that I am."

"You are. And you're also compassionate, otherwise we wouldn't be sitting here."

"Oh, no," Eden laughed, the sound rife with self-derision. "We can chalk that one up to stupidity."

"Ouch," Bennett said, only half joking, as the barbed comment found its mark. He'd been hoping to preface the apology with the "compassionate" remark, but clearly that hadn't worked. Was this the place for this conversation? Probably not, but Bennett had to take the opportunities where he could find them. So far, this had looked like his best bet, but…

"I'm sorry," Eden said, looking truly repentant. "That was ugly."

Bennett finished the last of his beer and signaled the waitress for a second. "No, I asked for honest, didn't I?"

"Still." She paused, a line of frustration emerging between her brows. "It's just… After everything that's happened between us, everyone is going to think I should have better sense."

"Than to see me again?" he asked. "This isn't a date—it's a business proposition."

She aimed her bottle at him. "It's a business proposition that I can't tell anybody about, which makes me look like a fool. Not that I mind," Eden hastened to assure him. "You've got a stalker, for pity's sake. I'm just sayin'…" She shrugged, letting the rest of the uncharitable sentiment left unsaid.

Bennett swallowed, the ramifications of his selfish plan surfacing, as usual, at an inconvenient time—as in, when it was too late to do anything about it. He'd been so desperate to spend some time with her, to make the case for his apology, that he hadn't stopped to consider how being seen with him in public was going to affect her. Ironic, wasn't it? He'd sworn her to secrecy about his stalker to protect his own hide and in the process had sacrificed hers.

He was pathetic, Bennett thought as his insides writhed with humiliation. Utterly pathetic.

Quite frankly, when he'd suggested that they get together tonight, he hadn't invited her to the house because he hadn't wanted his gimlet-eyed grandfather watching and listening to his every move. She'd suggested Ice Water, rather than her house, which would have suited him much better as they would have had some privacy.

No doubt that's why she'd suggested the bar and grill, and it just went to show him how desperately she hoped to keep him at a distance. He knew she wanted him—could feel it every time those gorgeous green eyes tangled with his. Could read it in the unwitting way she leaned toward him when they were together, as though she gravitated to him the same way he'd always gravitated to her. But she was willing to risk being the object of renewed ridicule to keep from being alone with him.

Now that was distinctly disheartening.

In fact, now that he thought about it… Bennett glumly reached into his back pocket for his wallet and tossed some bills on the table. "You know, this was a bad idea. I hate that I've—"

"What the hell are you doing?" Eden whispered urgently, leaning forward in her seat.

"Giving you an out."

Eden glanced around the room, then leaned forward even more, and though her lips were shaped into a smile, the dangerously chilly tone of her voice and the fire blazing from her eyes begged to differ. "If you get up from this table and leave me sitting here by myself before we even finish our meal—if you humiliate me *again*—I will tear those precious balls from your body and hand them to Artemis525 myself." She upped the voltage of her smile. "Am I making myself clear?"

Bennett stilled and the 'nads in question inexplicably shrank at her threat. Well, all righty then. "Are you sure?" he asked.

Eden huffed an exasperated breath. "You have a stalker, Bennett," she said as though he still didn't comprehend the gravity of the threat. "Of course I'm sure. Now sit back and tell me just exactly what it is you want me to do."

Fine, Bennett thought, more than marginally relieved. He'd hoped to work around to this by degrees, but since she was so adamant and had so eloquently cut to the chase, he'd tell her.

"I want you to come stay with me."

12

FLABBERGASTED, STUNNED, SHOCKED and otherwise bowled over, Eden snapped her mouth shut. "I can't come stay with you," she said, her voice a breathless squeak. "Have you lost your mind?"

"No," Bennett replied drolly. "I just thought the goal here was to save my life." His lips twisted. "My mistake."

"We can save your life without me moving in with you," Eden said, trying to remain calm. Jeez, Lord, as if she didn't have enough to worry about. Now he wanted to muddy the waters even more by having her stay with him? Twenty-four-seven?

Why didn't she just head to the bathroom with him now—it's not as though they hadn't done it there before, Eden thought, her pulse tripping at the merest thought—then tell him that she still loved him so that he could dump her all over again? The fast-forward version of each one of their courtships. Naturally she wanted him to be safe, but this—

This was out of the question.

"Look, Bennett, I'm going to do everything I

can to find out who she is before the twenty-fifth, but as far as actually *protecting* you…I don't know what I'd do exactly that you can't do for yourself."

He frowned thoughtfully. "Didn't you take some defensive training before you joined the police force?"

"Haven't you been kicking ass since kindergarten?" Eden shot back. She knew what he was doing—knew that, for reasons known only to him, he wanted to keep her close. This was just an excuse. Yes, he needed to take the stalker seriously, but keeping her in his pocket wasn't going to keep him any safer. Did she feel a bit responsible because this crazy woman was using a Web site she'd designed out of spite? Yes, but that didn't mean she was going to be an idiot.

Bennett smiled, blew out a resigned breath. "I'm not going to win on this, am I?"

"No," Eden said, barely suppressing her own grin.

"At least give me the twenty-fifth," Bennett pressed. "If you really think that's when she's going to make her ultimate move, then even you can't deny that you should be there."

Eden paused, examining her motives, silently considering the request. Given what she knew and what she expected, then yes, she had to agree that being with Bennett that night would probably be a good idea. If this were anyone else, she would certainly make that call.

She swallowed, then nodded cautiously. "Okay,"

she said. "And naturally, if anything happens, you should call me. I don't suppose you have any new ideas as to who it could be?"

Bennett shifted uncomfortably and hesitated, causing Eden's belly to flip over in dread. No doubt it was some new conquest he'd remembered, someone from town, no less, which was going to make her want to break things and cry. Eden steeled herself against the anxiety and irritation hurtling through her, and tried to focus. This was serious, after all. She couldn't afford to let emotions get in the way.

At least not right now. She'd cry later.

"Come on, Bennett," she told him. "If you've thought of someone, then you've got to tell me who—"

Bennett gave his head a small shake and looked away. "It's nothing, really. Just a far-out-there suspicion not worth mentioning."

"Bennett—"

The waitress chose that moment to deposit the hot wings on the table, momentarily preempting Eden's ability to press him further. Margie, twenty years older than him and married to boot, looked down at Bennett and smiled flirtatiously enough to set Eden's teeth on edge.

"Welcome back, Bennett," she said as though Eden wasn't sitting there. "I didn't know these were yours or I'd have put some extra ranch dressing on there for you."

Bennett shot Eden an uncomfortable look and actually blushed.

Bennett Wilder—*blushing*. Now there was something she didn't think she'd ever seen before. She knew Ben had come back from Savannah a different person from the one who'd left Hell, but clearly the changes were much deeper than what she'd realized. Eden filed the thought away for future contemplation. In the meantime…

"Evening, Margie," she said brightly, forcing the waitress to acknowledge her presence. "Now that you mention it, I'd like to have some extra ranch dressing." She smiled sweetly. "And another beer, if you don't mind."

Margie's grin turned a bit sick. "Certainly."

Bennett's twinkling gaze met hers once the waitress had walked away. "Am I mistaken, or did you just post a No Fishing sign."

"No," Eden said, feeling her cheeks pinken. "I just posted a 'Hey, what about me?' sign." She fidgeted in her seat and tucked her hair behind her ear. "Honestly," she sighed, rolling her eyes. "It's sickening."

Bennett grimaced. "It also gets old."

"Yeah, right," Eden scoffed. "Don't hate me because I'm beautiful, eh?"

Bennett helped himself to a wing. "I didn't say it wasn't flattering, I just said that it gets old."

In the process of dunking a celery stick into a pool

of dressing, Eden paused to look at him. She'd detected the smallest amount of disappointment in his voice, as though he'd regretted being honest with her. She swallowed, annoyed with herself on too many levels to enumerate. "I guess any sort of attention—be it good or bad—has the potential to get old."

Bennett looked up and something unreadable shifted in his gaze. "That's my take, anyway."

Eden released a shallow breath. "So…back to this new suspicion you think isn't worth mentioning—mention it," Eden said pointedly.

"I—"

Oh, for heaven's sake, Eden thought. "How am I supposed to find this girl if you won't give me the information I need?" Good grief, it's not as if she wasn't aware of his man-whore reputation. She knew, dammit. It sickened her, broke her heart, but it wasn't a damned secret. "You know, Bennett, I appreciate the fact that you're now embarrassed by your, er…womanizing reputation—and you seem like you want to change that—but you've picked an inconvenient time to go noble. I—"

Bennett passed a hand over his face and swore. "It's not someone I've slept with, dammit," he finally snapped, clearly not wanting to have this discussion. "Or even dated, for that matter." He shuddered, as though the mere notion made him want to wretch.

Eden blinked. The idea that this wasn't a scorned

lover had never occurred to her, and frankly she couldn't imagine anyone who hadn't had an intimate relationship with Bennett hating him enough to pose a threat. She frowned, confused. "I don't understand. Who exactly are you talking about?"

Bennett hesitated again. "Look, Eden. This isn't the place."

Eden lifted her chin. "This is the place we've got. *Tell me who she is.*"

Bennett paused to consider her, seemed to be bracing himself for some sort of fallout. Finally his lips twisted with bitter humor and he released a whooshing breath. "Your mother."

Eden froze and her entire body went numb with shock. "My mother?"

Looking miserable at having to have this conversation with her, Bennett shrugged awkwardly. "I told you we didn't need to do this here."

"My mother?" Eden repeated, dragging the word out.

"She certainly hates me enough, don't you think?"

She hated him, yes, but enough to threaten him? To stalk him? To hurt him? Surely not, Eden thought. She couldn't believe, couldn't imagine— Eden gave her head a skeptical shake. "I don't know, Bennett. She—"

He winced, clearly regretting saying anything to her about it. "Look, you pressed for it and I told you. I'm just saying…she wasn't above smashing that heart that I carved for you—" He paused and quirked a questioning brow.

Eden nodded, silently acknowledging that she remembered. God, did she ever remember.

"And she wasn't above coming to me and telling me that if I didn't stop seeing you, she'd make you pay. That she would make sure that *you* hurt and that it would be *my* fault." He tapped his bottle softly against the tabletop and curiously seemed unable to meet her gaze. "She can be pretty damned ruthless, and frankly I don't think her elevator goes all the way to the top."

Eden's mouth went bone-dry, her heart rate soared and an impending sense of dread hovered like a shadow around her shoulders. Her mother had gone to him? she thought faintly. Had told him that if he didn't stop dating her that she'd make Eden pay? That it would be his fault? Whereas only moments before Eden had been numb, feeling now came rushing back, making her entire body tingle. Nausea clawed at her throat, and anger and humiliation swirled through her churning belly with enough force to make her hold so tightly on to her fork that she could feel it bending in her hand.

That manipulative bitch, Eden thought. How could she have done something so terrible? So deceitful? Eden knew without having to ask that Bennett was referring to the first time he'd broken up with her, when they'd been in high school. He would have been too young to have fought back, wouldn't have known what to do. And he would have been too embarrassed to come to her and tell her why he was breaking up with her.

A bitter laugh broke up in her throat, and she shook her head as the impact of what he'd finally shared cleared up so many questions she'd had over the years. When they'd gotten back together the last time, Eden had been too elated to bring up any of the old problems they'd had. He'd apologized, and she, content with the sincerity, had merely accepted.

As always, she'd just wanted him. Even now, God help her, she wanted him. She could feel her body betraying her—an achy yearning in her sex, in the tingling tips of her breasts, the sluggish way her blood was moving through her veins. She could lie to herself and chalk it up to the alcohol—she'd always been a lightweight, after all—but Eden knew better. It was Bennett, had always been Bennett and always would be Bennett.

He finally cleared his throat, evidently uncomfortable with her extended silence. "I'm sorry, Eden. I should have told you a long time ago. I was just so ashamed of not fighting for you, and it was just easier to become what everyone had expected me to be."

"It's not what I expected you to be," she said softly.

A sad smile shaped his beautiful mouth. "I know."

"What did she say to you exactly?"

He shook his head. "It doesn't matter now. I just

thought, in light of my stalker, that you should know. What do you think? Could she be the one?"

It did matter, Eden thought, but she wasn't going to insist that he tell her. It had taken ten years and a stalker impetus to get him this far. Pushing Bennett didn't work. Besides, given the dark turn Bennett had taken, he didn't have to tell her for Eden to know what her mother had said to him. She could just imagine. Her mother had the rare ability to ferret out a weakness with pinpoint accuracy, then strike with even more chilling efficiency.

As for her being the one—who knew? Eden supposed it was possible. Considering Giselle's housekeeper did all the shopping, it would be easy enough to find out if she'd bought any chicken livers lately. She shared as much with Bennett.

"You'll keep me posted, right?"

"Sure," Eden said, releasing a small breath. And on that note, it was time to leave. She'd had all the walking down memory lane she could stand for one night. Any more and they'd be holding hands and kissing and having wild, frantic, wonderful, back-clawing, screaming-orgasm sex. She swallowed a whimper as a hard tingle pinged her sex. Eden reached for her wallet, but Bennett quickly stalled her.

"I've got it," he told her. "Give me a minute and I'll walk you to your car."

Eden summoned a smile. "I've had some self-defense training," she said, tossing his earlier observation back at him.

He grinned at her, recognizing the attempt at humor for what it was—a tension breaker. "And I'm trying to be a gentleman."

Eden slid out from the booth and made her way toward the exit. "Ah," she said knowingly. "Another part of the turning-the-whole-tree-over, eh?"

Bennett held open the door for her, snugging a finger at the small of her back, causing a delicate tremor to work its way through her. "One leaf at a time, babe," he sighed. "One leaf at a time."

Eden bit her lip against the tide of longing that rose inside her from that simple, innocuous touch. A blaze of gooseflesh raced up her spine, licked around her belly and settled between her thighs. She bit her lip against the instant invariable rush of tangled emotion and desire, the ultimate feeling of desperate longing she'd known only with him.

Sweet heaven.

Rather than remove his hand once they'd walked outside, Bennett kept it at her waist, making her all the more aware of him—which she wouldn't have thought possible. *Don't touch me,* Eden thought desperately. *If you touch me, I'll come unglued. I'll fall apart and back at your feet and you'll break my heart all over again. Don't apologize. Just let me go. Let me go.*

Just a few more steps and she'd be at her car and

she could escape before she did anything stupid. Eden released a shaky breath, reached for her keys and hit the remote lock.

Bennett stopped behind her. She could feel his gaze skimming her profile, could feel his regret and uncertainty pinging off of her like little miserable darts of remorse. Oh, God. *Time to go,* Eden thought, urgency making her almost fumble her keys.

"Good night, Ben—"

"I'm sorry, Eden."

Equally quiet, intense and sincere, those dreaded words left his lips and slipped right into her heart.

Eden closed her eyes tightly and stilled. There it was, she thought with a quiet laugh. Her downfall. The end of life as she knew it. She'd known it was coming, hadn't she? She wanted to tell him it was too little too late, to say that being sorry wasn't good enough.

She wanted to be angry at him for taking advantage of her vulnerability, but instead she was just angry at herself for not being able to stay strong. God help her, why couldn't she hold a proper grudge? Why couldn't she be as cold as Kelly? As angry as Kate? Why couldn't she hold on to a modicum of self-respect, self-restraint and self-preservation where Ben Wilder was concerned?

Why? Why? Why?

Eden knew why—he was her Ben. Her One. The only guy she'd ever loved and instinctively knew she'd ever love.

Gallingly, Eden felt tears burn the backs of her lids and she lowered her head, disgusted, miserable and ashamed of the weakness.

Bennett swore softly, then settled his hands on her shoulders and gently turned her around.

"Don't, Ben," she whimpered, more to save face than to really protest. She knew what he was going to do, knew what was to come and hated herself even more for wanting it when she knew she shouldn't.

He tunneled his big, warm hands into her hair, cupping her jaw, pulling a shudder of anticipation out of her that soaked her panties and made her nipples pearl behind her bra.

His dark, troubled gaze searched hers, then he breathed her name into her mouth as he settled his lips over hers.

For the briefest second Eden simply savored the feel of his lips meeting hers. Other than the softest sigh of inevitable heartache, she didn't respond. It was too perfect, too beautiful and more than she'd ever hoped for…being kissed again by Bennett Wilder.

Then need and instinct took over, and she wrapped her arms around his neck and greedily sucked his tongue into her mouth, because tasting him was more important than anything else in her world at the moment.

In fact, her world had shrunk to the point that it only included the two of them and the small patch of asphalt that currently anchored her feet to the pavement.

Feeling his hard body aligned thrillingly with hers, that sinfully carnal mouth feeding at hers as though she were a rare treat…that was all that mattered.

Bennett's strong fingers massaged her scalp and cradled her face. His breath was ragged, and little masculine sounds of pleasure reverberated off her tongue. The hot length of him nudged her belly, making her own sex throb to an intense beat that she hadn't felt in years. It was almost enough to make her cry.

Sweet sexual longing hurled like a caffeinated sugar rush through her body and concentrated in areas that had been neglected since he'd left town. Her breasts grew hot and heavy, her neck felt as if it was too weak to support her head and her spine seemed to have melted completely, because she was clinging to Bennett as though she were unable to stand on her own. Her blood burned sluggishly through her veins, making her a curious combination of lazy and energized, and a pressing itch commenced in her clit that made her wiggle shamelessly against him.

Seemingly reading her mind—or, more accurately, her body—Bennett lifted her up, pinned her against the car and rocked against her. The first hint of pressure ripped the breath from her lungs, and the promise of impending climax spiraled through her sex.

"God, Eden," Bennett growled, bumping against her once more.

God didn't have anything to do with this, Eden thought. This was the devil in her reacting to the devil in him, and were they anywhere but a public street, she'd be ready to commit some seriously overdue back-clawing, name-screaming *wonderful* sin.

Eden pressed herself more firmly against him, wincing as her achy nipples met the hard wall of his chest. Dammit, why hadn't she parked in the back? Then they could have simply crawled into the backseat of her car. *In for a penny, in for a pound,* Eden thought, not even questioning the fact that they were going to sleep together again. She'd known it was a foregone conclusion, hadn't she? That's why she'd tried to keep him from apologizing. She'd known—

"Hey! Get a room, why don't you!"

Breathing hard, Eden tore her lips from Bennett's long enough to watch a smiling Kelly Briscoe drive past. She shot Eden a thumbs-up, which drew a questioning look from Bennett.

Bennett frowned. "What was that all about?"

Mortified, Eden peeled herself away from Bennett. She'd just inadvertently scored one for the Ex-Girlfriends' Club, but she suddenly felt as though she'd made a terrible mistake. Then again, she'd made so many tonight, trying to pin one down seemed like too much trouble.

Kelly quickly forgotten, a lazy smile curled Bennett's lips and a sleepy-looking, all-too-wicked gleam flashed in those come-sin-with-me eyes. "I liked her suggestion," he said, blatantly fishing for an invitation back into her bed.

Eden weakened and wavered, and her body, having been spoiled and primed by Bennett's masterful kissing skills, staged a successful rebellion against her better judgment. Why fight it? she thought with an inevitable sigh.

Heartache now versus heartache later—either way she knew she was doomed.

At least this way she'd enjoy the road to ruin first.

Eden sighed and, smiling resignedly, jerked her head toward her SUV. "Get in the car."

13

Get in the car, Bennett thought four minutes later as he and Eden—her legs wrapped around his waist, her hot, hungry, equally desperate mouth attached to his—zigzagged their way through her darkened kitchen. Had more wonderful words ever been spoken?

"It's straight…through there," Eden told him between kisses. She pushed her hands into his hair, kneaded his scalp, setting his entire body aflame. "Last door on the right."

Hell, he'd done good to get out of the car. He hadn't thought they were going to make it inside at all, but the gearshift digging into Eden's hip had registered long enough to break the sexual haze and they'd managed to stumble through her back door.

Terrified that Eden would change her mind before they could get to her house, Bennett had kept up a selfishly wicked siege against her on the short drive over—he'd nibbled on her earlobe and slipped his hand between her legs, massaging her until she climaxed and jumped the curb coming into her driveway. Selfish? he thought, smiling against her mouth. Not completely.

But in this case the end would justify the means.

The minute they got inside the house he was going to be back inside her, and the need hammering throughout his body—the primal animal drive beating a relentless tattoo in his loins—told him that it couldn't be soon enough. He didn't just need her—he *had* to have her.

Hell, he'd never been able to keep his hands off her. They'd always—*always*—been hotter than hot together. Because they'd been each other's first? Bennett wondered dimly, and not for the first time. Learned together, as it were? Or was she simply his Achilles' heel?

More than likely all of the above.

Bennett nudged open her bedroom door, and the sweet smell of magnolia blossoms met his nose, a scent he'd always associated with her. The big, beautiful trees lined her parents' driveway and Eden had always kept a bouquet in her room. Clearly that hadn't changed. His tongue tangling around hers, Bennett cracked an eye open long enough to find the bed—a big Spanish antique that dominated the room—then made his way forward.

An unearthly yowl sounded above their heavy breathing, causing Bennett to almost trip and fall. Startled enough to call his badass reputation into question, he tore his mouth away from hers. "What the fu—"

Eden chuckled softly and dropped her head against his shoulder. "Cerberus."

Right, Bennett thought darkly. How could he forget? The cat currently sat in a ready crouch, every hair on its back standing on end, looking ready to pounce if Bennett so much as made a move. Evidently dear old Cerberus had been sleeping soundly, curled up on Eden's duvet before they'd arrived.

Clearly there wasn't enough room for both him and the cat in the bed. As if coming to the same conclusion, Cerberus growled and hissed low in her throat and inched forward, a feline dare.

Though he knew it was juvenile, Bennett hissed back, drawing a chuckle from Eden.

"Here," she said, wiggling down from him. "Let me put her out of the room."

"I don't think she's going to like that," Bennett said, eying the cat warily.

"Probably not." Eden lifted Cerberus off the bed and carefully set her outside the door, then pulled it closed with a finality that brought a smile to his lips. "But she'll get over it." Her hot green gaze raked his body from head to toe, making his skin burn. "Now where were we?"

Bennett pulled his shirt over his head, tossed it aside and dropped onto the foot of her bed. "We were working on getting here."

Smiling, Eden toed her shoes off, then coolly shucked her shorts, revealing lacy low-rise aqua-colored panties. Looking confident and in control—God, what a turn-on—she sidled forward, pushed him down and straddled him. She was tanned and toned and sexy as hell.

A halo of pale hair framed both of their faces as she lowered her mouth to his, bringing a fond smile to his lips. He'd always loved her hair, Bennett thought, feeling the silky mass slip over his cheek.

Growling, he cupped the firm roundness of her rump, aligning her against the hard ridge of his arousal, then slid his hands up her slim, supple spine. He knew every indentation, knew the exact measure between each vertebra, knew what sort of touch drove her wild and tripped her trigger.

He knew *her,* Bennett thought, his throat tightening, and he knew that he liked himself better when he was with her.

And what was even better…she knew him. Take now, for instance. She was sucking his tongue into her mouth—back and forth, back and forth—making him want her hot, talented mouth wrapped around his rod, sucking him until his balls ached and release rocketed from his loins.

Desperate for the feel of skin on skin, Bennett slipped his fingers beneath the hem of her shirt and tugged it upward. Eden shifted, allowing him to draw it over her head, then she sat back on her haunches, reached behind her back and undid her bra.

Bennett reached up and fingered the aqua lace—apparently part of a set—and felt his mouth parch with need. "Nice," he murmured thickly.

Pale blond hair shimmering over her shoulders, her green eyes darkened to a mossy hue, her lips swollen from his kisses, her pretty bra barely clinging to her heavy breasts…

Eden painted a picture in that moment that would forever be branded into his memory. She was so gorgeous it made his chest ache. Beautiful from the inside out.

"You're so beautiful," Bennett murmured, unable to keep the compliment to himself.

Eden's lips slid into a smile as she shrugged the rest of the way out of her bra. "Your flattery is wasted—you've got me in bed already."

Bennett chuckled. "Smart-ass."

Her mouth curved into a little half smile, Eden bent forward once more and licked a hot path up the side of his neck, sprinkled leisurely kisses along his jaw then kissed the corner of his eye. She sighed softly, fondly, as though she'd missed that particular part of him. Lucky for her, he had more parts and he was more than willing to share them with her, ad nauseam, should she so desire.

Her warm palms slid over his chest, mapping

Rhonda Nelson 179

him slowly and reverently, and he had the pleasure of watching her body go boneless with desire.

Unable to keep from tasting her, Bennett bent forward and pulled the rosy bud of her breast into his mouth, groaning with pleasure as the taste of her spread over his tongue. Eden gasped, tunneled her fingers into his hair and held him fast, anchoring him to her.

Fire licked through his body, settled in his loins and pushed his dick up so hard against his zipper that he winced. He couldn't wait to get inside her, couldn't wait to feel her sweet, greedy heat clamping around him, holding on to him.

And to that end…

He wanted to go slow, to take his time, to love her properly…but he couldn't. This was Eden, after all, and he'd never had any self-control when it had come to her. He'd never been able to adhere to any sort of seduction—he'd always just had to have her. Period. And from the little sighs of delight, the mewls of anticipation he was already wringing from her primed little body, Eden didn't appear any better at resisting him.

Thank God.

And considering they were in what used to be a church, he meant it literally.

Eden's clever hands suddenly found the snap at his jeans and he felt the clasp leave its closure. His zipper whined, and a second later her hot little palm was wrapped around his dick, milking a single bead of moisture from the tip.

Bennett tested the weight of her other breast against his hand, then moved over and sampled it, as well. Same flavor but better somehow, Bennett thought dimly, wondering if sexual attraction had somehow momentarily unhinged his brain.

Eden worked the slippery skin back and forth, back and forth, then multitasked by removing his pants and drawers with the other hand, slowly inching them down over his ass until Bennett could kick them away.

Then the only thing that stood between him and her was a thin patch of silky lace and his ultimate intentions. He'd been patient, Bennett thought. He'd let her hold on to the dominant position, but now it was his turn. He wanted her beneath him, hot and ready, wet and willing and just as desperate as he was.

In an instant he had her on her back.

She wrapped her legs around his waist and rocked up against him, wincing with pleasure. Her eyes fluttered shut, her mouth rounded and a needy sigh leaked out of her lungs.

The drenched lace between her legs slipped over his dick, making him jump impatiently against her. It felt curiously nice, better than he would have expected but not good enough. A broken gasp erupted from his throat.

Not nearly good enough.

Bennett nudged her panties aside and pushed up through her wet, hot folds, purposely nudging her clit.

Predictably, Eden's back bowed off the bed. A wicked, almost sleepy-sounding chuckle of relief bubbled out of her ripe mouth, making Bennett want to beat his chest and roar.

Him, he thought. She wanted him.

Still.

He slid through her folds again, drenching himself in her heat, then went painfully still as thought struck. Son of a bitch.

Eden's questioning gaze tangled with his. "What's wrong?"

"I don't have a condom."

"You don't have a—" Eden blinked, seemingly astounded. "*You* don't have a condom?"

In her mind, he imagined, it was a bit like van Gogh not having a paintbrush, but what could he say? He hadn't had good sex since Eden, and the bad sex had gotten old quickly. He grimly suspected that she'd ruined him, but there you go. There was nothing for it.

Bennett shook his head, felt his lips twitch into a small smile. "Haven't needed them until now."

Something shifted in her gaze and it softened perceptibly. Then she smiled and rocked her hips back, positioning him at her center. "Don't worry about it. I'm on the pill."

A weight of relief rushed through him, seemingly plunging him inside of her.

Hot, tight, wet...*home.*

Bennett lodged himself so deeply inside of her, he felt her lungs deflate as he buried himself to the hilt. She clamped around him, squeezing him tightly, making climax kindle threateningly in his burning loins.

"Eden," he breathed, bending down to brush a kiss over her lips. "God, I've missed you."

Home, Bennett thought again as he thrust again, then he wrapped an arm around her waist, hauled her hips closer to his and pounded into her.

Home, home, home and *mine, mine, mine.* Prayer or plea, the Almighty could take his pick. He just needed her.

14

EDEN CLUNG TO BENNETT, absorbed the force of his thrusts with greedy anticipation. She wrapped her legs around his waist, savoring each and every hardened inch of him deep inside of her.

It was so perfect she could almost cry.

This was what she'd been missing, Eden thought as profound relief mingled with desire, making her go alternately boneless and rigid. Emotion clogged her throat and crowded into her heart, and the backs of her lids burned even while a goofy, giddy smile turned her lips.

There was nothing quite so perfect as the feel of Ben Wilder buried to the hilt between her legs. It was hot and thrilling and wild and wicked—just like him—and if she'd ever felt anything more perfect in her life, she couldn't recall it. But it was always like this with Bennett. He made every cell in her body sing, every particle in her being hum like a tuning fork.

The minute he'd pushed into her it was as though the rest of her world had fallen back into place. Everything settled…then flew apart again when he started to move.

In a move of brazen wickedness, Bennett had massaged her to climax in the car on the way over to her house—while she'd been driving, of course. That had to be against the law, Eden had thought dimly at the time, but she hadn't had the wherewithal to tell him to stop. She'd barely been able to get out of the car—and probably wouldn't have been able to without his help. Getting the key in the lock had been a challenge, as well, because he'd picked her up and had been nibbling on her neck.

Heaven help her, but he smelled good, Eden thought now, inhaling the clean woodsy scent of him. He'd undoubtedly showered before meeting her in town, but Eden could still catch a whiff of oak. She bent forward and kissed him, the exact spot where shoulder met neck, tasting the salty essence of his skin against her tongue.

Predictably, Bennett hardened even more inside of her.

"Eden," he said warningly.

Smiling, she nipped at his shoulder, then licked the spot she'd bitten. "I'm busy," she told him, sliding her hands over his chest, raking his hardened nipples with the smooth edge of her fingernails.

"I know," he said, a broken laugh bubbling out of his throat. "You're killing me."

"Then rigor mortis has only settled in one part

of your body," Eden quipped, chuckling at the inane joke.

Bennett grinned down at her, deliberately thrust harder and seated himself as firmly between her legs as he could. "Nice form, but your comedic timing is a little off."

Eden rocked against him, purposely catching his rhythm, and felt the quickening of climax tingle in her sex. "Then I guess I'll just have to work on that, won't I?" Eden said, her voice suddenly hoarse with need.

Bennett upped the tempo, pounded into her—harder, faster, then harder still. She felt his balls slap her aching flesh, watched his lips peel away from his teeth and knew he was about to come.

And there was nothing more beautiful than watching Ben Wilder when he came.

Though desire dragged her lids down and tension tightened every muscle in her body, Eden locked her legs tighter around Bennett and gazed determinedly up into his woefully familiar, handsome face. She would not look away, didn't want to miss a single expression.

Almost as if he'd read her mind, he looked down at her, and the desire—the sheer unadulterated need—he allowed her to see in those remarkably dark eyes sent Eden over the edge.

The climax hit her with only the slightest of warnings. Her feminine muscles clamped around him, holding him inside of her with each pulsing quake. Her back bowed off the mattress, her neck arched away from the bed, her mouth opened in a soundless scream and her vision blackened around the edges. Every cell in her body sang with release, throbbed in her weeping sex, and every push of him deep inside her felt exaggerated—bigger and better than before.

Her orgasm seemingly triggering his, Bennett thrust wildly into her. Pounded harder and harder. A fine sheen of sweat slickened his shoulders, every perfectly proportioned muscle rigid with tension. Masculine art in motion.

Then it happened.

She felt him stiffen, dig his toes into the mattress and nudge deep, then felt his warm seed bathe the back of her womb, igniting another little sparkler of pleasure deep inside of her. Unable to help herself, Eden smiled contentedly.

Sweet peace, she thought, silently praying it would last a little longer this time.

Breathing heavily, Bennett narrowly avoided collapsing on top of her. He wilted and rolled to the side, taking her with him. His lips curled into an endearingly sexy smile and he pressed a kiss to her temple. "Well, I don't know about you, but I feel better."

Still trying to catch her own breath, Eden slung her arm over her eyes and chuckled softly. "I all but screamed your name and you have to wonder if I feel better? If you're fishing for a compliment, then—" *Oh, what the hell,* Eden thought, laughing "—damn, that was good."

He doodled on her upper arm. "Yes, well," he said, masculine pride dripping with every syllable. "I can't take all of the credit," he said magnanimously. "You did some of the work."

Eden chewed the inside of her cheek and turned to look at him. His dark hair was tousled in careless waves around his face and his eyes sparkled with latent humor and sated need. He looked sleepy and content and…happy, Eden thought with a surprised start. Not just satisfied but genuinely *happy*.

"I'll try to do better about pulling my weight next time," Eden said, regretting the words the instant they'd left her mouth. It implied that there was to be a next time, and while she certainly hoped there would, who knew with Bennett? She hadn't dubbed him the Magician for nothing. Just because he was back in town permanently didn't mean that he couldn't just as easily dump her and vanish from her life as he had before.

As if reading her mind, Bennett leaned over and placed a lingering kiss on her lips. "Next time I won't be so impatient that I leave your panties on." His gaze drifted up her wall, toward the ceiling, and narrowed. "Your cat is a pervert," he said darkly.

"What?" Eden followed his gaze and discovered Cerberus on the wall above them. She smiled, feigning insult. "My cat is not a pervert. She's merely curious."

"She can't jump down from there, can she?" Bennett asked suspiciously.

Worried, was he? Eden thought, smiling. "No. That's part of the reason I left the walls at eight feet, though. She likes to climb. She can get on top of most every ledge, but can only get down in a couple of places. She's not brave enough to jump."

Cerberus hunkered low and growled at Bennett, seemingly prepared to refute that claim.

"Maybe she's just never been properly motivated," he told her, eying the cat with suspicious disdain.

"Lay off my kitty," Eden admonished. "She's a sweetheart."

"She's a demon from hell. Maybe I should bring my dog over so that they can play."

Eden brightened. "You have a dog?"

"No, but I'm going to get one." He glared at Cerberus. "The biggest, meanest one the local animal shelter has to offer."

"Bennett," Eden said, whacking him playfully on the chest, causing a laugh to rumble against her cheek. Even though her cat clearly didn't like Bennett, she knew he was just teasing.

"I *am* going to get a dog," he said matter-of-factly, shooting her a look. Not asking her permission, of course, but…gauging her reaction, maybe? What, did he think she thought he wouldn't make a good pet parent? She knew Bennett had worried about being a good parent in the past—bad blood, he'd told her many years ago—but surely he didn't still believe that, Eden thought. It was ridiculous. He could be good at whatever he set his mind to and no doubt would be a wonderful father, to both the two-legged and four-legged varieties.

"Really?" Eden asked, encouraging him with the simple question.

"Yeah." He sighed. "I couldn't have one at my place in Savannah, and I like having the company when I'm working."

Eden could easily see that. Cerberus was quiet company and a source of comfort for her. She'd actually wanted a dog, as well, but she spent so much time away from home she wasn't altogether sure it would be fair to the animal. Cerberus, for all her faults, was quite independent.

"What does Grady think about you getting a dog?"

Bennett slid her a smile. "He'll warm to it."

Eden paused, felt a grin move over her lips. "You haven't told him, have you?"

"No, and I'm not going to. It's going to be a surprise."

Considering that Grady was a retired mail carrier who'd been chased and bitten multiple times, Eden didn't think Bennett's grandfather was going to appreciate his surprise. But who was she to meddle? "I'm sure that'll make a difference," she remarked drolly.

Bennett hesitated. "Can I ask you something, Eden?"

Intrigued at his cautious tone, she nodded. "Sure, but I reserve the right not to answer."

"Duly noted." He cleared his throat, shifted a bit. "Look, no one is happier than me that you're on the pill, but…why?"

Eden sucked the insides of her cheeks and resisted the natural impulse to say, *Hi, Pot. Meet Kettle.* However, the fact that he'd wondered and was sufficiently jealous enough to inquire made her inwardly preen. "Generally, it's taken for birth control," Eden told him. "But I'm on it to regulate my cycle."

He expelled a little breath of what she could only conclude was relief. "I was just curious," he said as though her answer hadn't mattered. But it had.

"Sure."

Bennett glanced at her bedside clock and winced. "I guess I should be heading back. Devi will have left hours ago, and I don't like to leave him for too long."

The true seriousness of his situation hit home to her in that moment. She'd known, of course, that he'd moved back to take care of his grandfather, but she hadn't truly put it into perspective—*his*—and realized all he'd given up in order to make that happen. He'd uprooted himself from a successful life in a place where he was accepted without ridicule or censure…and relocated back in Hell.

To repay a debt and care for the aging grandparent who'd taken care of him when the chips were down. The citizens of Hell could say what they wanted about Bennett—and, sadly, most of it was true—but deep down, where it counted, he was a good man.

"I'm not blowing you off, Eden," Bennett hastened to assure her when she failed to respond quickly enough.

Eden gave her head a small shake. "No, I didn't think you were. I was just thinking about how hard it had to be for you to give up your life in Savannah and move back here."

Bennett carefully disentangled himself from her, then leaned forward and brushed a warm, slow kiss over her lips. "It's been hell," he admitted. His sexy gaze tangled with hers, then drifted almost lovingly over her face. "But it just got better."

Her stupid heart absorbed the comment and pulled her mouth into a dawning smile. "We should get going," Eden said.

Bennett's gaze drifted to the wall, getting a careful read on Cerberus. "Can she get in the bathroom?"

Eden rolled her eyes. "No. It's right through there," she said, pointing him in the appropriate direction.

After a quick trip to take care of necessary business herself, Eden dressed and drove Bennett back down to his car. They'd no more than turned onto Main Street when Grady called and put in an order for a dipped cone from the Dairy Cow.

Bennett smiled fondly and closed the cell. "He's like a little kid, but with more attitude."

Eden chuckled. "A dipped cone, eh?"

"With nuts."

"Ah," Eden said, pulling in next to Bennett's car. "That's always better." She shifted into Park, suddenly unsure of what to say or do next. This was the part where things had always fallen apart for them. She got her hopes up, he dashed them, she was brokenhearted, etc….

Bennett leaned over and traced a gentle half-moon on her cheek, then kissed her with enough heat to let her know that he definitely wasn't sick of her just yet. "Thank you, Eden," he said, his voice thick with sincerity.

"For what?"

"For…*everything,*" he said, heaving a grateful sigh. "Giving me a break I didn't deserve. Being with me tonight. Taking care of this whole stalker thing," he said, smiling. "I've, uh…I've missed you."

And there it went, Eden thought, mentally watching her heart land right back in the palm of Bennett's hand. As if he hadn't always had it…because he had. Eden released a slow, stuttering breath. She'd been in love with Bennett Wilder since she was eighteen, and no amount of heartache, time or distance had ever changed that. And on some level she'd always know that it never would. He was her Ben, her greatest weakness, biggest comfort and soft place to land. *Until he pulled another vanishing act,* a sly little voice needled. Until he decided she was disposable again.

Eden looked away, over his shoulder, making a futile effort to find some much-needed perspective—then something odd caught her eye.

She frowned. "Bennett…what's that on your car?"

A line emerged between his dark brows. "On my—" He turned and peered out her passenger-side window. "Oh, shit," Bennett said, opening the car door. "Something that doesn't belong there," he said, his face blackening with anger.

Dread landing a blow to her midsection, Eden exited the car as well, and joined Bennett next to his BMW.

"Son of a— What the hell is up with this chick and meat?" he asked, his voice climbing.

Someone—Artemis525, no doubt—had smeared hamburger all over the driver's-side window of his car. It had puddled into a coagulated mess in the crease of his window and dripped down the side of his car.

"If she left the meat, she left the note," Eden told him. She peered around him and found it tucked beneath the wiper blade. Eden carefully opened the envelope and inspected the message. *"Maybe I'll run your heart through a meat grinder after I'm finished with it. You're between the crosshairs now."*

Bennett swore again and looked around, evidently wondering if she was out there now, watching them. He pushed a hand through his hair and swore again. "Dammit, I hate this," Bennett told her. "I feel so damned helpless. I feel like she's toying with me, like she's getting a charge out of making me crazy." His cell rang again. He checked the display, closed his eyes tightly shut and sighed deeply. "What, Gramps? Yes, a dipped cone. With nuts," Bennett said through gritted teeth. "Yes, I know. No, nothing's wrong. No, it's not. *No. It's not,*" Bennett growled, shooting her an embarrassed look. "I'll be home soon."

Eden waited until he ended the call. "You aren't going to tell him?"

"Nah," Bennett said, shaking his head. "No sense in him worrying. We know when she's going to strike. We've just got to be ready for her." He said the last with a chilling determination that made Eden's pulse trip.

"We will be," Eden told him, letting go a shaky breath. She'd been spooked from the start, but this was getting decidedly worse. "Are you sure you don't want me to talk to the chief? Because I can ask him to keep it on the q.t. and—"

Bennett shook his head. "No, Eden. Please," he added. "I've got you. We can handle it."

She hesitated. Something about this felt wrong, but she couldn't exactly put her finger on it. "If you're sure?"

"I'm sure." Bennett pressed another vein-singeing

kiss to her lips, then pulled away and clicked the keyless remote, unlocking his doors. "I'll call you tomorrow," he said.

Time to throw down the gauntlet, Eden thought. "For what?"

He paused, shot her a guarded look. "What do you mean, 'For what?'"

Her stomach knotted with uncertainty, Eden cocked her head and felt a shaky smile curl her lips. She just wanted to know where she stood this time, that's all. If this was going nowhere—if she'd been an itch he needed to scratch—then she wanted to know that *right now,* before things went any further. Considering their history, she didn't think it was too much to ask.

"For business or for personal reasons?" Eden asked, lifting her chin.

Something shifted in Bennett's gaze, a resolve that she'd never seen before. It was as if he'd come to some sort of decision, one he didn't verbally share but that sent a thrill of hope winging through her chest all the same.

Bennett took two quick, determined strides forward, kissed her so hard it drove her head back, and she melted against her car. Hot, deep, drugging and wicked, he made a promise with his mouth, one she could taste, one she could feel as if he was chan-neling it into her. It seeped through her skin and into her blood, pounding out a rhythm that matched her dreams and made her wish for things she'd never spoken of aloud.

A life with him, a future with him, dark-haired children and sleeping late on rainy days.

"Oh, it'll be personal," Bennett assured her when, breathing heavily, he finally pulled back. "Does that answer your question?"

Eden struggled to catch her breath, pressed a trembling hand to her still-tingling lips and cleared her throat. "Er…yes," she said in a voice she barely recognized, it was so small. "Yes, it does."

Bennett nodded succinctly, seemingly pleased with himself. "Good. I'm glad we understand each other."

Her, too, Eden thought faintly. In fact, if they'd understood each other any better at the moment, she would have undoubtedly had her third orgasm of the night. She smiled. One for each year he'd been gone.

But they still had a lot of making up to do…provided Artemis525 didn't kill him first.

15

DESPITE THE SMEARS OF hamburger on his car and a lunatic woman threatening to rip his heart from his chest and run it through a meat grinder, Bennett found himself curiously upbeat and energized.

Because of Eden.

He watched her pull away, her long blond hair shimmering in the moonlight, and felt a tug of emotion so intense it snatched the air from his lungs. Tonight had been…perfect. Being with Eden again was like the first breath after a near drowning—fulfilling on so many levels he'd actually ached with the happiness of holding her again, feeling her sweet little body clutching his. Those small capable hands kneading his scalp, tunneling through his hair, wrapped around his rod. And that first thrust into her body, being baptized in her heat…

Mercy.

Bennett didn't know when anything—other than being with her before—had ever felt more right. He loved the way he felt when he was with Eden. He felt taller, bigger, better somehow. She made him want to be his very best, to rise above his humble beginnings and let go of the pain of his past.

She made him want to *love* her, not just *make love* to her.

Dangerous territory, he knew. He'd come to the same conclusion three years ago and, to his eternal regret, he'd walked away from her.

But not this time. This time he was going for the brass ring, and to hell with anyone—including her mother—who thought he wasn't good enough.

She thought he was good enough, dammit, and ultimately hers was the only opinion that mattered. He would not run scared this time. He would not let her down. He was offering his heart up to her this go-round and, though it might only be wishful thinking on his part, he thought Eden wanted it. Why else would she have sought reassurance of his motives? He'd known when she'd asked him why he planned to call her tomorrow what she'd wanted to know. She'd wanted to know if this was just sex. Just another quick fix like the last time when he hadn't been able to keep his hands off her.

And it wasn't. Sometime between the minute he'd sat down to dinner with her tonight and the moment he'd stepped out of her car he'd realized that he wasn't settling for a mere portion of Eden—he wanted all of her. Did he deserve a third chance? No. Did he deserve her? Bennett shrugged.

Probably not. But he wanted her anyway, and if that made him a selfish bastard, then so be it.

But better a selfish bastard with her than a lonely one without.

Bennett pulled through the Dairy Cow drive-through and picked up Grady's dipped cone, then made his way back out to the farm.

Surprisingly, Devi's car was still in the drive. Why the hell had Grady rushed him home if Eden's aunt was still here? Bennett wondered, slightly annoyed. Bennett let himself in the back door and found the two of them in the living room watching *Jeopardy!* "Take Ancient History for two hundred, stupid," Grady barked at the screen.

"Now that's why you always lose," Devi told him. "You should go for the big money. Go for a thousand. Sure, the answers are tougher, but if you're not smart enough to answer them, then you don't have any business being on the show."

"You're such a know-it-all," Grady told her, scowling. "It must be hard carrying around all that knowledge."

Devi harrumphed. "Since your old knobby head is filled with air, it must be considerably easier to haul around yours."

"My knobby head?" Grady repeated angrily. "I'll show you a—"

Bennett cleared his throat loudly.

Both Devi and his grandfather turned to face

him, the picture of innocence. "Bennett," Devi said. "We didn't hear you come in."

That much was obvious, he thought, flattening a smile. He sidled over to his grandfather and handed him the ice cream.

"Nuts?" Grady bleated, outraged. "Did I ask you for nuts?"

Bennett felt his blood pressure ease up a notch. "As a matter of fact, you did."

Grady frowned skeptically, as though he doubted the credibility of that claim. "Whatever. I'm just glad that you're finally home." He sent him a shrewd glance. "You know, if you're gonna start dating, we're gonna have to have some rules."

Bennett didn't know what to address first—the fact that his grandfather thought he could mandate his dating habits or the fact that technically he and Eden hadn't been on a date. It had turned into one, of course, but considering her aunt was sitting in his living room watching him with curiously sharp eyes, Bennett didn't feel like discussing it.

"Here's a rule," he said tiredly. "Mind your own business."

"All I'm saying is that you can't be dallying with Eden." His grandfather scowled. "She's a good girl, and according to Devi here, you haven't treated her with the respect she's deserved."

Bennett shifted uncomfortably, unable to refute

that claim. His uneasy gaze slid to her aunt's. "I'm not dallying," Bennett told her. He cleared his throat. "And I've apologized for my past mistakes."

Devi peered at him consideringly, then finally nodded. "I should get going," she said, rising gracefully from her chair. Until that moment Bennett had never noted the similarities between her and Eden. There was a certain peace about the two of them, a knowing sort of glow and mischief that twinkled from their eyes. A similar carriage and charm.

She paused. "Is something wrong, dear?"

Bennett gave his head a small shake and rubbed the back of his neck. "No." He shot her a look. "I just realized how much Eden favors you, that's all."

Devi smiled. "Much to her mother's resentment, I can tell you."

That was hardly surprising, Bennett thought, barely suppressing a derisive snort. What did Eden's mother not resent?

"You know Giselle once had a thing for your grandfather, don't you?" Devi asked him, her eyes twinkling with humor and something else, something he couldn't quite define.

Grady snorted. "She's a witch. I never had anything to do with her."

Thank God, Bennett thought, astounded. Giselle? Chasing his grandfather? A Wilder?

"Eden's mother and I are nothing alike," she said, smiling mysteriously. "For instance, she's really good at holding a grudge. Funny how families are like that sometimes, though." She picked up her purse and sighed softly. "Oh, well. You know what I'm talking about," she said as if she and Bennett understood each other. "I knew both of your parents and yet I don't see either of them in you."

Bennett stilled, absorbing the offhand comment.

It was true, he realized. Parents or not, he was nothing like them. Granted, one could argue that he'd inherited his mother's whoring tendencies. But, in all fairness, he was a man, and men typically tried to get laid with as much frequency and furor as possible. His lips quirked of their own volition. He'd just been more successful at it than most. And in recent years, even that had grown old.

As for his father, Bennett had never had a problem with alcohol. He knew his limits and he respected them. Frankly, while he enjoyed a good buzz, getting hammered had never really appealed to him. He liked being in control of his actions, didn't like dulling his senses beneath a haze of alcohol. Furthermore, he'd always—even at his worst—had a good work ethic. Kirk Wilder had held a job long enough to drum up liquor money, and that had been it.

He *wasn't* like them, Bennett realized with the sort of *aha* clarity that made him rock back on the balls of his feet.

He was his own man, responsible for his own

actions and destiny…and, thanks to Eden, he felt as though his destiny had just taken a turn for the better.

Maybe living in Hell wasn't going to be hell after all.

"I FORBID IT."

In the process of fastening her belt around her waist, Eden paused and looked at her mother as though she'd lost her mind.

And clearly she had, or she wouldn't have arrived on Eden's doorstep this morning tossing around mandates and laws to which she had no authority.

"You don't have the right to forbid it," Eden told her. "Because it's none of your damned business."

"None of my business?" her mother countered shrilly. "My daughter has been seen in public with a low-life heathen—"

"Bennett is neither a lowlife nor a heathen." Eden paused. She really didn't have time to get into this right now—she was running late for work as it was—but since her mother was here… "He told me what you did," Eden told her, barely keeping her voice even.

Giselle wrinkled her nose and picked a cat hair off her pant leg. "Told you what?"

"That you made him stop seeing me. That you told him if he didn't, *you* would hurt me and it would be *his* fault. How dare you?" Eden asked, her voice cracking with anger.

Her mother smirked. "It was for your own good. He would have ruined you."

"That was not for you to decide then, any more than it is for you to decide now."

"I was only looking out—"

Eden cut her off with a hard glare. "Don't even say it," she said. "Don't tell me you were looking out for me. It's a lie and we both know it." Eden smiled without humor. "The only person you have ever cared about is the one you see in the mirror every morning. You didn't want me seeing him because he didn't measure up to your standards. Well, news flash, Mother. He didn't have to. He had to measure up to *mine*."

Giselle merely smiled, then stood. "Then you need to raise your standards."

"And you need to mind your own business."

In the process of fishing her keys from her purse, her mother paused to look at her. "Ah," she said knowingly. "I see I'm too late. He's already set the hook again, has he?" She strolled to Eden's front door. "I'm disappointed in you, of course—I'd hoped you'd have better sense—but I'm not worried." She paused. "History is wont to repeat itself. He'll cut bait soon enough."

And with that parting shot, Giselle made her way out the front door.

That barb finding a mark, Eden moved to the window just in time to watch Cerberus chase her mother from the yard. "Good kitty," she said, smiling in spite of herself as she rested her head against the glass.

As always, her mother had managed to hit upon the one thing Eden was terrified of—that Bennett would "cut bait" again. Last night, when she'd driven away, she'd been so certain that things were going to be different this time. She'd felt a security with him last night, which, frankly, she'd never experienced before. She'd been hopeful in the past, but…this was different. This Bennett was more sure of himself, more confident, seemed to have a better grasp of who he was.

Devi would tell her to ignore Giselle, to follow her heart. Devi would tell her to trust her instincts, even if that meant she was wrong. Eden grinned. It wasn't as if her aunt hadn't been through this with her before. Still…doubt was a shadow she was having a hard time shaking. She wanted to believe in him, she really did. But she was just so terrified of being made a fool of again, of giving up her heart once more and of him vanishing out of her life the same way he had in the past. True, he was trying to turn over that tree, but did that apply to her, as well?

Eden's cell rang, cutting off her circling thoughts. A quick check of the display told her it was Kate.

"So…how's it going?" her friend wanted to know. "Kelly e-mailed the club and told them that she'd seen you and Bennett kissing outside Ice Water last night. Is that true?"

"It is," Eden admitted.

"So, whose house did you go back to? Yours?"

"What makes you think we went to anyone's house?" Eden asked, her cheeks warming guiltily.

Kate chuckled. "You forget who you're talking to, sweetie. I *know* you. Bennett Wilder is your ultimate weakness. He's to you what coconut cream pie is to me. If I see a slice, I've got to have it."

Though she was late for work, Eden collapsed into a nearby chair. "If you knew that, why didn't you come to my rescue?" she demanded. "Why did you let me get badgered into breaking Bennett's heart?"

Kate let go a long-suffering sigh. "Are you going to do it?"

"Of course not."

"Precisely," Kate told her. "But getting with him again was inevitable. At least this way you look like you have an excuse."

Eden frowned, not altogether sure she liked Kate's uncharitable logic. "You're quite evil," she said. "Are you sure that *you're* not Artemis525?"

"That's another reason I called. She's been quiet on the board. Has anything else happened?"

Eden filled her in on the hamburger incident as well as the 525 suspicions. "I really feel like I might be in over my head here. I need to go to the chief, but I promised Bennett that I wouldn't."

"That's a promise you don't need to keep. This is getting worse and worse."

"I know," Eden said, rubbing her forehead tiredly. "It's a mess. I'm not exactly sure what I'm going to do."

"Well, you don't need to be there on the twenty-fifth, that's for sure. You've got to get him out of the house."

Actually, she'd already thought about that and had planned to take him up to Fire Lake to pass the time in a way they'd both enjoy. Kate was right. Staying in that house like a sitting duck wasn't a good strategy. Someone—namely an officer of the law—needed to be posted outside Bennett's house. Once again she relayed her concerns to Kate.

"Get him to agree to it," her friend told her. "Be *persuasive.*"

Eden chuckled softly.

"You okay?" Kate asked, concerned. "Seriously."

"I'm scared," Eden admitted. "But—" She shrugged helplessly even though Kate couldn't see her. "It's *Ben,* Kate. It's always been Ben."

Kate made a sympathetic sound in her ear. "I know, honey. Just be careful, okay?"

Eden nodded. "I will."

But it was too late for that, Eden thought as she disconnected. She'd already put too much of herself out there to be anything but honest now. Eden whimpered.

And she honestly wanted *him.*

16

"So this is the biggest, meanest dog you could find at the animal shelter, eh?" Eden asked with a droll smile as his newly adopted pet ran in hyper circles around her leg, yapping playfully.

Bennett sighed. "Nope." He waited until Vicious lumbered into the room, then pointed at the gigantic dog. "*This* is."

Seemingly confused, Eden looked up from the delightful puppy at her feet, then her gaze landed on Vic. Her eyes widened in apparent shock and she stumbled back a step in alarm. She looked from the puppy to Vicious, then to him. She raised her brows. "You adopted *two* dogs?"

"Yes, he did," Grady said. "Wasn't that nice?" he asked with mock happiness, when it was plainly obvious that he thought it was anything but nice. "He said they were a surprise for me." Grady's dark brown eyes regarded the puppy with beleaguered irritation, then he rattled his paper and disappeared behind it once more. "Just more things to take care of around here. As if I've got time to toddle around behind a couple of dogs," he grumbled.

"Oh, put a sock in it," Devi told Bennett's grandfather. "They'll be good company for you."

"I don't know what *you're* so happy about. You're the one who's going to be cleaning up after them."

"Vic is housebroken," Bennett told them. His gaze slid to Addie, and he frowned. "Addie's gonna need some work."

"Oh, she's a smart one," Devi said, patting the puppy on the head. "You won't have any trouble with her."

Bennett didn't think so, either. He'd actually gone to the shelter to adopt one animal but had ended up coming home with two. Puppies were generally adopted first because they were cute and cuddly and adorable. Naturally that's what Bennett had wanted, but one glance at the morose-looking Vic—probably one of the biggest, ugliest dogs he'd ever seen—was enough to stop Bennett in his tracks. The animal had been dumped, the clerk had told him, and his days were numbered.

A sucker for a sad case, Bennett had made sure the animals were going to get along, then packed them up and brought them home. Vic tolerated Addie's enthusiasm with the sort of stoic you-have-no-idea resolve that was pure entertainment in and of itself.

Eden's gaze darted between the two dogs. "Are you sure Vic isn't going to eat Addie?"

"They were cell neighbors," Bennett explained. "They've bonded. She was the runt of the litter, he was headed for the big fire hydrant in the sky." He pulled a shrug. "They both needed a home."

"Ah," Eden said, evidently touched. "You did a good thing."

Bennett smiled and absently rubbed his chest. "Sometimes I get a wild urge."

"Speaking of wild, I heard you had an interesting day today," Devi interjected, smiling knowingly.

Eden rolled her eyes. "It was an experience, if nothing else."

Intrigued, Bennett felt his brow fold. "What was an experience?"

"Eden had to fish Martha Warren out of the mud puddle again."

Fish Martha Warren out of the mud puddle again? Bennett thought, thoroughly confused. He pulled a frown. He vaguely remembered doing a job for Ryan at the Warrens' place. "Martha Warren. Isn't she in a wheelchair?"

Devi smothered a chuckle behind her hand and her eyes twinkled with undisguised mirth. "She is. Oh, Eden, I know I shouldn't laugh. It's terrible, it truly is, but—"

Grady cackled. "But it's damned funny, too," his grandfather finished for her.

Eden, too, looked as if she were having a hard time keeping a straight face. Her ripe lips trembled, seemingly trying to keep from laughing. "Be that as it may," she said, "it's still terrible. And it was time Johnny got a dose of his own medicine."

Still confused, Bennett shook his head. "What am I missing here?" he asked, wanting in on the joke.

Eden cleared her throat. "Martha *is* in a wheelchair," she confirmed. "And almost every time it rains, when Johnny gets angry at his wife, he rolls her outside—against her will, I might add—" Eden stopped and pursed her lips again, forestalling another smile "—and d-dumps her into a big pothole in their driveway."

Bennett felt a disbelieving smile roll across his lips and a you're-kiddin'-me laugh break up in his throat. "No?"

"Yes," Eden confirmed with a single nod. "None of the other guys on the force will go out there and help Martha because I'm the only one who can do it with a straight face…and she has a tendency to rarely wear a bra."

Bennett seemed to remember that about her.

"My sources tell me that you might have fixed the problem permanently, though," Devi said, shooting Eden a sly look.

A slow smile curled Eden's lips. "I don't know

about permanently, but I think he'll think twice before he does it again."

Grady's bushy brows formed an intrigued line. "What did you do?"

"I hit him with the stun gun, rolled him into the hole then sandbagged him."

Bennett felt his eyes round, and he almost choked. "You what?"

Eden pulled an unrepentant shrug and humor danced in those clear green eyes. "Turnabout is fair play. I didn't hurt him," she said. "I just needed to change his perspective."

Impressed, Bennett nodded thoughtfully and regarded her with open amazement. "You're devious," he said, grinning.

Eden smiled, evidently pleased with the assessment. "But I'm also fair. Martha needed someone to level the playing field for her." She lifted one slim shoulder in a negligent shrug. "So I did."

"Have I mentioned how grateful I am to have you in my corner?" Bennett asked.

A cloud of unrecognizable emotion flashed momentarily in her gaze, causing Bennett an instant of disquiet, but she blinked it away before he could get a firm read on it. "You're welcome," Eden told him. Her lips slid into a smile, but there was a forced quality to it he didn't altogether understand. "So…" she said, looking curiously anxious. "Are you ready to go? The chief should be here soon."

Bennett considered her for a moment, then gave himself a mental shake and tried to focus. Contrary to his wishes, Eden had finally badgered him into allowing Mitch Curtis, the chief of police, to come out and watch the house. Tonight was the night, after all, the dreaded 5/25. She'd sweetened the deal with a trip to Fire Lake—*their place,* Bennett recalled, his dick hardening at the mere thought—and since Mitch had always seemed like a stand-up guy, Bennett had ultimately let himself be persuaded. Mitch had promised to be discreet, and in exchange Bennett had offered to make his wife a rocking chair.

True to form, Grady had proved to be a pain in the ass and had absolutely refused to leave the house. And when Bennett had tried to point out the safety concerns, his grandfather had blistered his ear with expletives that would have made a sailor blush. This was his house, Grady had maintained, and he wasn't leaving.

They were taking Eden's SUV and leaving Bennett's car here at the house to perpetuate the illusion that he was home. Since there was no way to know exactly when she'd make her move, Devi had offered to spend the night—under the guise of not missing out on the action, of course; otherwise his grandfather would blow a gasket. Mitch had assured their safety, so Bennett had finally acquiesced.

Fire Lake, Bennett thought. *With Eden.*

Talk about a little piece of heaven here in Hell. His gaze drifted over her face—the smooth curve of her softly rounded cheek, the fine line of her nose, the sleek, curiously vulnerable slope of her brow. Clear green eyes, bright with humor one minute, then mossy with desire the next. His chest inexplicably tightened with emotion, crowded his heart up into his throat, forcing him to swallow.

Was he ready to go? Bennett thought, releasing a slow, uneven breath.

Hell, yes.

Because he was already a goner.

17

HAVE I MENTIONED HOW grateful I am to have you in my corner?

Eden inwardly squirmed.

She really needed to tell him what the Ex-Girlfriends' Club had asked her to do—to admit her duplicitous part in it—but somehow hadn't been able to drum up the nerve. Things had been too wonderful between them over the past couple of days, and she'd been too much of a coward to rock the boat or put a chill on their bliss. Was it so wrong to want to hold on to a little happiness?

Furthermore, it wasn't as though he'd always been particularly forthcoming with her. She just wanted a little more time, a better footing, so to speak, on where they stood. She thought they'd found solid ground this time, but...

Kelly, Marcy and Sheila had cornered her yesterday in town and had wanted to know when they were going to get to do their big "reveal." Evidently they had some sort of "punked" fantasy scenario for Bennett wherein they *all* let him know how she'd deceived him. Eden had swiftly disabused them of that notion—good Lord, what were they thinking? Had she actually gone through with this, how could they expect her to be so cruel? Honestly, it was incomprehensible. She'd started this, she'd told them, and she'd finish it.

In her own way. In her own time.

Meanwhile, at some point she was going to have to come clean with them, as well. Too many confessions, Eden thought, feeling her head begin to ache.

"Is something wrong, Eden?" Bennett asked. The afternoon sun painted him in an almost sepia glow as it descended below the horizon, making her breath catch in her throat. He had rolled his window down, and the breeze it created tousled his hair, giving him a curiously boyish charm. Almost there, Eden thought, turning onto the rutted dirt drive which would take them up to their spot above the lake.

She smiled reassuringly. "No. I'm just worried about all this Artemis525 stuff," Eden said, not quite lying. She *was* worried about it, though admittedly it hadn't been the focus of her recent preoccupation.

"She's been quiet the last couple of days," Bennett pointed out, smiling weakly. "Maybe she's found someone else to stalk."

"I don't know," Eden said, frowning thoughtfully. "Something about this has felt weird to me from the beginning, but I can't put my finger on it." She shook her head. "I'm probably overthinking it."

Bennett leaned over and nuzzled her neck, his warm breath making a delicious shudder work its way through her. "Maybe you just need something to take your mind off it," he murmured silkily, instantly conjuring images of all the ways he intended to do that. And if it was anything like the way he'd done it the past couple of nights—though they'd been short ones due to Grady's care—Eden knew what was in store for her.

Mercy.

Yesterday afternoon he'd been waiting for her at her back door when she'd finished her shift. Looking like the wonderful badass that he was, he'd been leaning against her house, one foot kicked up behind him. He'd exuded a sexy wickedness and charm that had made her tingle in anticipation before she'd even gotten out of the car. She'd opened the door to her kitchen, then he'd followed her in and backed her against it.

Fifteen seconds later she'd been half-dressed and hotter than hell, absolutely mad for him. Cerberus had made her usual unhappy appearance, but Bennett had merely turned, glared hard at her and growled, "I'm sticking around. Get used to it."

By the time he'd left, Eden had been weak-kneed, wrung dry and otherwise sated in every way possible, and Cerberus had been winding around Bennett's legs, purring contentedly. Eden grinned, remembering.

"Your kitty likes me now," he'd said, stroking the shameless feline on the head.

"My kitty has always liked you. It was my cat who found you offensive."

Bennett had laughed, the beautiful wretch. God, she was a head case, Eden thought. She was so miserably head over heels in love with him she could barely remember her own name. And she had to have a new one by the end of the month, she thought, grimacing at the reminder. She'd shared that predicament with Bennett as well. He'd been tossing names at her left and right, but so far nothing had really appealed to her.

Eden backed her SUV up into optimum viewing position. Bennett met her at the back, opened the rear gate of her car and they settled side by side into the roomy cargo area. *Ah,* she thought, *just like old times.* They'd timed it perfectly. Fire Lake glowed like its name as the setting sun shimmered out over the water. Ducks floated near the shore, and birds hovered just above the water's surface, looking for dinner.

"This never fails to take my breath away," Eden said quietly, awed by Mother Nature's glorious display. She felt Bennett's hand slip into hers and squeeze.

"Mine, either," he whispered softly, though he wasn't looking at the lake—he was looking at her.

A warm flush of pleasure settled over her heart and a dart of pure joy landed in her chest. The raw emotion she heard in his voice, saw in his eyes, made her desperately want to believe that what they had was real, would last, would survive whatever insecurities Bennett had allowed to ruin their previous shots at happiness in the past.

She wanted him so desperately—not just physically, though that was certainly a perk. She wanted to go to sleep with him at night and wake up with him in the morning. She wanted to fight over breakfast and make up with a nooner. She wanted to hold hands and watch movies, share holidays and French fries. She wanted him at his best, at his worst and all species in between.

Sitting here now, just looking at him, made her ache with the want. She felt it in every particle of her being, deep in her bones. Ben Wilder was her missing piece, her soul mate, her one and only and her hero. And for tonight, Eden thought as his thumb skimmed her bottom lip, he was hers.

"Penny for your thoughts," Bennett said, leaning in to brush a reverent kiss across her lips. Eden's lids fluttered shut and she smiled softly.

"My thoughts are worth more than that," she murmured. "And they can't be bought—they have to be earned."

Bennett's grin was so slow in coming it would have rated an easy ten on the wicked scale. "Guess I've got my work cut out for me then."

Eden framed his face with her hands, skimmed

his cheeks with the pads of her thumbs then pressed a gentle kiss to each of his eyelids. "I have confidence in you," she murmured, smiling.

A deep, sexy chuckle vibrated up his throat, then bubbled into her mouth as he suddenly settled his lips over hers. He nudged her back, gently following her down, and Eden silently thanked the presence of mind she'd had to tuck a couple of pillows and a blanket into the back. At some point tonight she imagined they would go back to her place, but given the Artemis525 situation, who knew? Eden had her cell ready and waiting, and had extorted a promise out of Devi to call her the minute something happened. Knowing what Eden had planned, she was certain she wouldn't hear from her aunt until Bennett's stalker made an appearance.

"I have a good feeling about him this time," Devi had told her. "I'm pulling a different vibe."

Eden had, as well, and the fact that Devi had picked up on it made her feel slightly better, not quite so foolish for taking the risk again. He deepened the kiss and she felt the resulting tug deep in her achy womb. As if she'd ever had a choice to start with, Eden thought with a rueful smile.

She'd never been able to resist him. And thankfully she didn't have to pretend to anymore.

Especially now.

Eden had planned to take things slow, to make love to him with sweet emotion. Unfortunately, now that they were here, she didn't think she was going to be able to pull that off. A simple kiss from Bennett and she was already hovering on the verge of climax, wincing with pleasure as her panties abraded her sex.

"I'm making an executive decision," Eden told him, sitting up once more.

Bennett blinked. "What?"

She pulled her shirt over her head and cast it aside. "Get naked."

A rumbling laugh eddied up his throat, and a spark of challenge lit those wickedly sexy dark brown eyes. "You want me to get naked?"

Eden popped the front clasp on her bra and tossed it at him. His eyes fastened greedily on her breasts, and she had the pleasure of watching them blacken further with need. "Yes."

A beat slid to five, then Bennett leaned back and casually threaded his fingers behind his head. "I think I'm going to need a little persuading."

Oh, really, Eden thought, shooting him a look. He wanted persuading? Fine. She'd persuade him. She kicked off her shorts and panties, then straddled him. The first brush of his jeans against her sensitive flesh made her gasp and made Bennett's jaw clench until she thought she might have heard his teeth crack. Smiling, she slipped her hands beneath his shirt and mapped his belly and chest, paying particular attention to his nipples. His, she'd discovered years ago, were equally as sensitive as hers.

Bennett made a strangling noise and shifted up against her, pressing the hardened length of him against her needy sex.

That wouldn't do, Eden decided.

She found the button of his pants and slipped it from its closure, purposely letting her hands drift over the engorged head of his penis rising from his waistband. She wiggled lower, almost even with his belly button, and sighed dramatically. "I could play with this so much better…if you were naked," she added pointedly.

"Fuck it," Bennett growled. "I'm no good at playing hard to get." He sat up and pulled his shirt from over his head and tossed it aside, then shucked his pants and briefs with deft efficiency.

Eden wrapped her hand around his pulsing shaft, then lowered her head and took the whole of him into her mouth. "No, you're not," she agreed, licking him lazily. "You're much better at just being *hard.*" Smooth as silk, he felt fabulous beneath her tongue, the taste of him blooming into her mouth.

Bennett bucked beneath her and his thighs tensed. "Eden," he growled warningly.

Still eating him—licking, laving and savoring every incredibly hard inch of him—Eden glanced up, his throbbing rod in her mouth, and her gaze tangled with his. The black flame of desire burned from his eyes, making her impossibly hotter. Her sex weeped, her nipples ached and the need to settle herself firmly on top of him grew with each passing second. She ran her tongue over the engorged head, sucked up the bead of moisture leaking from there, then smoothly scaled his body once more.

Bennett, hot and hard and ready, anchored his hands at her hips and thrust upward, sliding between her folds, drenching himself in her juices. The head of his penis bumped her aching clit, making her breath hitch in her throat. Reading her, he bumped her again, effectively snatching the air from her lungs.

Desperate for release, Eden shamelessly pushed herself harder against him, braced her hands on his chest and absorbed the feeling. God, he was beautiful. Dark, dangerous, wicked...*hers.* Hands down the most beautiful, sexy man she'd ever seen.

She scored his chest with her nails, then lifted her hips and impaled herself upon him. Her vision flickered and her belly deflated in a whoosh of surprised air. *Sweet heaven,* Eden thought, as indescribable pleasure bolted through her.

Bennett's lips peeled back from his teeth and a guttural growl of male approval rolled out of his throat. He flexed beneath her, nudging her core.

Eden lifted her hips once more, then slid down the length of him, savoring every inch, every vibration between their joined bodies. But it wasn't enough. She wanted more, needed more. She rode him harder, up and down, up and down, faster and faster because she could feel the orgasm hovering just out of reach. She wanted, she needed—

Naturally, Bennett knew exactly what she needed.

He caught her rhythm, then bent forward and pulled her nipple deep into his mouth, causing an invisible thread between the two to contract. Eden felt the first spark of climax ripen in her sex. She tightened her feminine muscles around him, pumped harder and harder, creating a delicious drag and draw between their bodies. Evidently realizing that she was hovering on the edge of a violent orgasm, he flexed harder beneath her, then reached between them and massaged her clit.

She flew apart.

Eden's mouth opened in a soundless scream and her back arched tightly from the shock of release. She was suddenly boneless. Bennett kept up the tempo beneath her, and every powerful thrust of him deep inside her intensified the contractions. Impossibly, he seemed to grow even more, and each hot, electrifying inch magnified her own pleasure.

She heard Bennett's breath catch, felt him go rigid beneath her. Then a low, keening growl tore from his throat, and three hard thrusts later he joined her in heaven. A shock of warmth pooled against the back of her womb, sending another sparkler of pleasure through her.

Eden collapsed against his chest, listened to the

frantic beat of his heart beneath her ear and felt the reciprocating pulse still lodged deep inside of her. There was something so elemental, so indescribably perfect about being with him now, at this particular time, at this specific place.

Bennett wrapped his arms around her, then pressed a kiss to the top of her head. His breathing evened out and she rolled off him, then cuddled in next to his side. Contentment saturated every pore as the sun slipped completely beneath the horizon, bringing twilight.

"I didn't think I was good enough," Bennett said in the ensuing silence. Though the comment was matter-of-fact, Eden discerned the pain beneath it.

"Ben," Eden breathed, her heart aching for him. She'd suspected as much, but hearing him say it, knowing that he cared and trusted her enough to open himself up like this… She swallowed, a lump welling in her throat.

Finally.

"Your mother had told me that I was nothing. And for a long time—too damned long—I became what she said. I let her rob me of my self-worth," he said bitterly, clearly disappointed for allowing himself to be so manipulated and belittled.

Eden sat up, her gaze pinning his. "Oh, Bennett. It was never hers to take."

"I know that now," he told her, his voice rough with emotion. "But it's been a long and winding road I would have rather traveled with you."

Eden pressed a kiss to his cheek, then searched his gaze and smiled. "I'm not going to argue with you there, but...we seem like we're on the right track now."

Bennett's warm gaze melted with relief, and a soft smile played over his mouth. "I've got something for you," he said, reaching beside him to pull something from his pants pocket. To her unending delight, he withdrew a small wooden heart identical to the one he'd carved for her all those years ago, the one her mother had destroyed.

Emotion clogged her throat, and the backs of her eyes burned as he held it up for her to see. "Ben," she breathed, touched more than she could have ever imagined.

"It's my heart," he said, an endearingly unsure smile curling his lips. "I know this is a bit hypocritical, but...don't break it."

Bennett fastened it around her neck and she settled in against him once more. "I won't if you won't," she told him, her chest tingling with warmth and happiness.

He hugged her tightly, and for the first time in her life her future seemed secure, brighter somehow. Because Bennett was going to be in it on a permanent basis.

"No worries," Bennett sighed. "I've turned over the whole tree, remember?"

18

"NOTHING?" BENNETT ASKED, quirking a brow a little while later. They'd napped and kissed, then made love again. He'd gotten a little glimpse of his future tonight and it looked like…heaven, Bennett thought. Anywhere with Eden couldn't be anything less.

Eden winced and shook her head, then flipped her phone closed. "Mitch says everything has been quiet." Her lips rolled into a droll smile. "With the exception of your grandfather and my aunt, that is. They got a little rowdy during *Jeopardy!*"

Bennett chuckled, unsurprised. He suspected there was something more than a little rowdy going on between Eden's aunt and his grandfather but didn't want to voice his suspicions until they were confirmed. He blew out a breath. "So…what should we do?"

Eden shrugged into her shirt and shot him a smile that made his groin flood with heat. "Why don't we head back to my place and do each other again?"

A bark of laughter erupted from his throat and his gaze tangled with hers. "That sounds *doable*."

His stomach rumbled and he slid her an embarrassed smile. "Do you mind if we eat first?"

Grinning, Eden shook her head. "Not at all. Does Ice Water work for you?"

"Sure."

Ten minutes later they were sitting in a booth in the back. Bennett reached across the table and threaded Eden's fingers through his. He'd never been able to keep his hands off her, but now…something had changed, he thought. The physical attraction had always been beyond anything in his experience. Touching Eden was better. Kissing Eden was better. Making love to Eden was better. Simply breathing the same air with Eden was better.

But being with her now, there was a permanence about it, a certainty that made his heart lighter, his chest inflate with warm, fizzy air. He was no longer a prisoner of Hell's perceptions, but rather he'd been liberated by his own. There was something to be said for coming into his own and knowing that Eden had been waiting for him on the other side.

He loved her, Bennett thought, amazed that the idea no longer seemed doomed or impossible. In fact, it seemed…destined. Preordained even. Fanciful? Maybe. But right now he felt as if the world were his oyster and he was getting ready for a lifelong feast.

With her.

Eden's eyes sparkled with fond humor and she

rested her chin in her palm. "Why are you looking at me like that?" she asked.

"Like what?"

Blushing, she pulled a light shrug and emitted a soft sigh. "I don't know. It's just a look I haven't seen in a long, long time."

He remembered, Bennett thought—the night he'd given her the first wooden heart, he'd told her that he loved her. Maybe he needed to remind her. Bennett leaned forward, poured every ounce of feeling he could into his gaze and shared it with her. "I—"

"Back here!"

Bennett frowned and shot a look over his shoulder. Kelly Briscoe, looking inordinately pleased with herself, was making her way toward their table, the rest of the Ex-Girlfriends' Club right at her heels.

Bennett glanced at Eden, who'd blanched. "Eden?" he asked, concerned. "Are you all right? Do you think it's her?" Was Kelly Artemis525? Bennett wondered. Eden had theorized that the threat hadn't originated from the club, but from the ashen look on her face, clearly she'd been wrong.

She swallowed and looked at Kelly. "Don't do this, Kelly," she said.

"Oh, but you're the one who's done it," Kelly enthused. She turned and rallied support from the rest of the group, then considered Bennett for a moment. "And done it quite well, by the looks of things."

"No, I haven't. I've—"

Bennett didn't know what the hell she was talking about, but if she was the chick who'd been driving him crazy, he was about to share a little of the insanity with her. He still hadn't gotten all of the damned hamburger meat off his Beemer.

Kelly turned her hard gaze to Bennett. "Are you in love with her?" she asked, jerking her head toward Eden.

"Bennett, don't—"

"Yes," Bennett said. This wasn't exactly the romantic moment he'd planned, but he wasn't going to deny it. He did love her. More than anything.

Kelly smiled again, seemingly pleased. "Good. Then we were right and our plan worked."

Bennett felt a cold chill land in his belly, and his gaze darted to Eden, who'd gone unnaturally still. "Your plan?"

"Tell him, Eden," Kelly told her. "Tell him how we nominated you to reel him back in, set the hook and then break his heart—the same way he's always done to us." Her triumphant gaze hardened. "Poetic justice, don't you think, Bennett?"

The chill turned to stone and dropped to his feet, rooting him to the spot. Hope withered and his world darkened. Little pieces suddenly fell into place. *The first night he'd gone to Eden's, they'd been there, plotting. Kelly shouting at them to get a room, then shooting Eden the thumbs-up.*

A bark of humorless laughter erupted from

his throat as he scanned the group of women around him. Curiously he didn't see Kate, whom he'd thought would want to be in on this moment. Though they looked a little uncomfortable, not a single one of them uttered a protest or refuted Kelly's claim—most damningly of all, Eden.

It certainly held her signature leveling-the-playing-field style.

Bennett fished a few bills out of his wallet, tossed them onto the table and shook his head. "The joke's on me, ladies." Though it took every ounce of will-power he possessed, he forced his lips into a smile and aimed it at all of them, most importantly Eden. "Well done."

Then, before she could respond, he slid from the booth, squared his shoulders and walked away. He'd endured worse, Bennett told himself, feeling like the ultimate fool. He couldn't recall when at the moment, but it would come to him. Besides, it was almost comforting. After all, he'd expected nothing less from Hell.

He met a harried-looking Kate on the way out and he bared his teeth in a smile. "Too late," he told her. "You missed the show."

Frowning, Kate hurried past him and into the bar.

IT TOOK EDEN APPROXIMATELY thirty seconds to fully comprehend what had just happened, and by that time Bennett had already made his exit.

She jumped from the booth, shoved past Kelly and hurried after him. She ran into Kate on her way out. "I'm sorry, Eden," Kate told her, looking miserable. "I tried to stop her."

"Go explain to them," she said, jerking her head toward the back. "I've got to find Bennett." He couldn't have gotten far, Eden thought. He didn't have a damned car. And there was still the matter of a crazy woman looking out there for him tonight.

She hurried up Main, fear and adrenaline and shame rushing through her with every quickened heartbeat. She should have known this would happen, dammit. When had Kelly, the bitter bitch, ever let anything go? Jeez, God, this was all her fault. She should have leveled with him, should have told him the truth days ago, but she'd been too caught up in being with him again—loving him again—to run the risk of ruining their time together.

Right up until this evening—until he'd handed her that wooden heart and told her not to break it— there'd been a niggling doubt in the back of her mind as to whether they would *really* make it this time. She'd wanted it, of course, and had wanted to believe it. But old habits die hard, and she'd been more familiar with Bennett-the-magician than Bennett-turning-over-the-whole-tree. Was it so terrible that she hadn't wanted to spoil any of their time together by revealing how petty her friends were, not to mention her part in it?

Eden spotted him up ahead and ran harder. "Bennett!"

He didn't slow down, didn't even acknowledge that he'd heard her. "Dammit, Bennett, *stop!*" Eden shouted.

Something in her voice must have reached him, because he finally halted near a streetlight. "What?" he drawled. "Want to come rub some salt in the wound?"

Eden finally caught up with him, then bent at the waist and sucked in some much-needed air. A stitch pulled in her side, but she forced herself upright. "No," she gasped, looking up at him. Pain lined his face and disappointment rounded his shoulders, making her ache for him. "You know me better than that."

He looked away, as though the sight of her hurt too much to bear, and his jaw worked angrily. "Is it true?" he asked. "Did they ask you to do that?"

"They did."

He smirked and chuckled darkly. "And what did you tell them?"

"I told them I would—"

Another bark of dry laughter broke from his throat and he turned and walked away again.

"But I never intended to do it. Surely to God you know me better than that."

Bennett stopped, turned around and stared at her. His troubled gaze bored into hers, anchoring her to the pavement. "I thought I did. But given your idea of justice…" He shrugged, leaving the rest unspoken.

Eden chewed the inside of her cheek and crossed her arms over her chest. She could feel Bennett's wooden heart nestled between her breasts, and the thought brought tears to her eyes. "There is a difference between justice and purposely hurting someone for the sheer sport of it, Bennett." She let go a breath and looked away. "Look, I'm sorry. But if you think that's what this has been about, then…I don't know, maybe it wasn't a good idea after all." *Liar!* a little voice screamed.

Bennett swore, kicked a rock at his feet. "I love you, dammit. It *was* a good idea. It's the best damned idea that's ever happened to me." He shook his head, rubbed a hand across the back of his neck. "I'm just…"

Eden sidled forward and wrapped her arms around his waist, breathed a silent sigh of relief as he settled his arms around her shoulders. "Terrified," Eden supplied for him.

Bennett looked down at her, his dark gaze rife with churning emotion. "Yeah," he said thoughtfully. "I am."

She chuckled softly and pressed a kiss to the underside of his jaw. "Welcome to my world, baby," she told him. "Me and fear are old friends. The heavy bitch sits on my shoulder every time you walk away."

She felt Bennett draw back and he peered down at her again. In that instant Eden knew he *got it*. He finally understood. "I'm sorry," Bennett said softly. "Really, truly, desperately sorry."

Happiness bloomed over her heart, pushing a smile to her lips. "And I really—" she kissed his cheek "—truly—" then his eye "—desperately—" and finally his mouth "—love you."

Bennett kissed her deeply, pulling a groan of pleasure from her body. He tasted like joy and home, good mornings and better nights. He tasted like…*hers*.

"Can you take me home?" Bennett asked, nuzzling her jaw.

Eden smiled against his lips. "Oh, yeah. That's *doable*."

Epilogue

"So what scared you more?" Grady wanted to know. "The chicken livers or the hamburger meat?"

Gathered at Ice Water for Eden's naming ceremony, Bennett peered around his grandfather and Devi and searched the crowd for Eden. "Er...I don't know. They were both pretty damned gross."

Devi released what sounded like an exaggerated huff. "Well, you have to pick one," she insisted. "One of them had to have scared you more than the other."

Bennett didn't know why this was so damned important. Ever since they'd arrived, Devi and Grady had been badgering him about Artemis525 and her threats. Ultimately she'd never made her promised move—which he was eternally grateful for, particularly as he was happier now than he'd ever been in his life. Instead, Artemis525 had posted to the message board that she'd heard that Bennett had learned his lesson and his imminent demise was no longer necessary. It had been as odd as her other posts, but frankly Bennett had just been glad the whole damned business was finished.

He had too many other things to focus on. Namely his fiancée, who'd disappeared the moment she'd walked through the door.

"Chicken livers or hamburger meat?" Grady demanded. "Pick one."

Annoyed, Bennett finally heaved a breath. "Fine. The hamburger meat," he snapped.

Grady cackled with joy. "I told you," he crowed to Devi, who for reasons that escaped his immediate understanding was scowling at him. "I told you the boy didn't like raw hamburger meat." Grady poked himself in the chest. "That one was my idea," he said proudly.

Bennett paused and frowned. His gaze darted between the two of them. He knew there'd been more to them than met the eye—and he and Eden had caught them in the act, in the living room, no less, when they'd returned home on the twenty-fifth. Eden had been shocked to learn that Grady had been her aunt's secret lover all these years, but Bennett had caught on relatively quickly. They bickered too much to be anything less than head over heels in love.

"What do you mean that was your idea?" Bennett asked, another suspicion taking root.

"You never really had a stalker, dear," Devi confirmed. "We just wanted to give you and Eden a little nudge."

Flabbergasted, Bennett felt a disbelieving smile slide over his lips. "What?"

"Ah," Devi said, looking past his arm. "There's my niece. I need to go ask her about her name." Eden's aunt frowned. "She hasn't shared it with me yet."

Unless she'd picked one since they'd walked through the door this evening, she hadn't settled on one yet, Bennett thought. He smiled.

Other than taking his, of course.

"You're not mad, are you?" Grady asked once Devi had moved out of earshot.

Bennett shook his head. Of course not. How could he be, when their lunatic machinations had resulted in the greatest happiness he'd ever known? He was marrying the love of his life in a little over a month. He'd settled into Hell mostly without incident and found that his grandfather had been right—perspective had changed things.

With the exception of Kelly Brisoe—who would never forgive him because she didn't want to—each and every one of the members of the Ex-Girlfriends' Club had shamefacedly apologized to him for their part in his humiliation. His "bastard" mug shot had been removed from the Web site, and the new design—which would not feature him in any shape, form or fashion—would be going up soon.

Eden's mother had uttered only a tight-lipped congratulations upon hearing about their engagement, but her father had shaken his hand and told him he looked forward to having him for a son-in-law. He'd been sincere, which had meant surprisingly more to Bennett than he would have imagined.

"So here's the thing," Grady told him, interrupting his thoughts. "I reckon me and Devi's going to go ahead and tie the knot, as well."

Bennett blinked, then felt a slow smile spread across his lips. "That's great, Gramps. I'm happy for—"

"We were kind of hoping that Eden would sell her place to us. You and Eden take the farm. It's bigger, after all. Better for raisin' a family, and you got your barn to work in."

Bennett swallowed, humbled by the offer. "You'd do that? You'd live in town?"

"I think I'd like it," Grady told him. "Being right in the heart of things, a block away from the square and all."

He and Eden had already been thinking about a permanent living solution and had actually talked about building near the farm. But actually having it…that was infinitely better. Bennett slung an arm around his grandfather's shoulders. "I'm sure Eden will be thrilled with the idea. Thanks, Gramps," he said, his voice going a bit rusty.

"You're welcome," Grady told him. "You're a good man and I'm proud of you."

Thankfully Eden chose that moment to stand on a bar stool in the center of the room and garner everyone's attention. Otherwise close inhabitants would have noticed that badass Bennett Wilder had just been moved to tears.

"Good evening, everybody," Eden called out above the din. "Thank you so much for being here at my naming ceremony. This has been a long-standing tradition of the Darlaston women—one I admire. But I have to tell you, choosing my name has been sheer hell." She smiled and ducked her head. "In fact, it only just occurred to me a few minutes ago."

A chuckle eddied through the room at this admission, and Bennett caught her mother scowling. Devi, on the other hand, merely smiled fondly and shook her head.

"When choosing a name as an adult, one has to really give it some special thought. Am I a Sophie? No. Lisa? No. Penelope? No." She paused. "If you think about it, it's pretty damned hard. But, after years of agonizing contemplation, I have finally chosen…Athena."

The room erupted in applause and Eden waited for it to fizzle out before speaking again. "You all know me to be fair," Eden told them. "But if the old adage that with age comes wisdom holds true—" her gaze drifted to Bennett and lingered "—then I've certainly wised up lately."

A knowing chuckle moved through the room and significant glances darted between him and Eden.

"So," Eden said, "while you are all here, I'm

going to share another secret." Her gaze tangled with his, pinging him with her love and excitement. "I'm not just adding a middle name next month. I'll also be changing my last name—to Wilder."

A series of delighted ohs, catcalls and general goodwill moved through the room, enveloping him like a warm blanket.

Eden hopped down from the bar stool and made her way to him. Smiling, she wrapped her arms around his waist, then looked up at him. Her clear green eyes sparkled with his future—love, joy, desire. Everything he'd ever wanted but never dreamed he'd have.

"What do you say we sneak off to the bathroom for a few minutes?" Eden asked him, jerking her head toward the back.

Bennett grinned wickedly. "I'd say that's doable."

* * * * *

Mediterranean Nights

Join the guests and crew of Alexandra's Dream,
*the newest luxury ship to set sail on the
romantic Mediterranean, as they experience
the glamorous world of cruising.*

*A new Harlequin continuity series
begins in June 2007 with
FROM RUSSIA, WITH LOVE
by Ingrid Weaver*

*Marina Artamova books a cabin on the luxurious
cruise ship* Alexandra's Dream, *when she finds
out that her orphaned nephew and his adoptive
father are aboard. She's determined to be
reunited with the boy…but the romantic
ambience of the ship and her undeniable
attraction to a man she considers her enemy
are about to interfere with her quest!*

Turn the page for a sneak preview!

Piraeus, Greece

"THERE SHE IS, Stefan. *Alexandra's Dream*." David Anderson squatted beside his new son and pointed at the dark blue hull that towered above the pier. The cruise ship was a majestic sight, twelve decks high and as long as a city block. A circle of silver and gold stars, the logo of the Liberty Cruise Line, gleamed from the swept-back smokestack. Like some legendary sea creature born for the water, the ship emanated power from every sleek curve—even at rest it held the promise of motion. "That's going to be our home for the next ten days."

The child beside him remained silent, his cheeks working in and out as he sucked furiously on his thumb. Hair so blond it appeared white ruffled against his forehead in the harbor breeze. The baby-sweet scent unique to the very young mingled with the tang of the sea.

"Ship," David said. "Uh, *parakhod*."

From beneath his bangs, Stefan looked at the

Alexandra's Dream. Although he didn't release his thumb, the corners of his mouth tightened with the beginning of a smile.

David grinned. That was Stefan's first smile this afternoon, one of only two since they had left the orphanage yesterday. It was probably because of the boat—according to the orphanage staff, the boy loved boats, which was the main reason David had decided to book this cruise. Then again, there was a strong possibility the smile could have been a reaction to David's attempt at pocket-dictionary Russian. Whatever the cause, it was a good start.

The liaison from the adoption agency had claimed that Stefan had been taught some English, but David had yet to see evidence of it. David continued to speak, positive his son would understand his tone even if he couldn't grasp the words. "This is her maiden voyage. Her first trip, just like this is our first trip, and that makes it special." He motioned toward the stage that had been set up on the pier beneath the ship's bow. "That's why everyone's celebrating."

The ship's official christening ceremony had been held the day before and had been a closed affair, with only the cruise-line executives and VIP guests invited, but the stage hadn't yet been disassembled. Banners bearing the blue and white of the Greek flag of the ship's owner, as well as the Liberty circle of stars logo, draped the edges of the platform. In the center, a group of musicians and a dance troupe dressed in traditional white folk costumes performed for the benefit of the *Alexandra's Dream*'s first passengers. Their audience was in a festive mood, snapping their fingers in time to the music while the dancers twirled and wove through their steps.

David bobbed his head to the rhythm of the mandolins. They were playing a folk tune that seemed vaguely familiar, possibly from a movie he'd seen. He hummed a few notes. "Catchy melody, isn't it?"

Stefan turned his gaze on David. His eyes were a striking shade of blue, as cool and pale as a winter horizon and far too solemn for a child not yet five. Still, the smile that hovered at the corners of his mouth persisted. He moved his head with the music, mirroring David's motion.

David gave a silent cheer at the interaction. Hopefully, this cruise would provide countless opportunities for more. "Hey, good for you," he said. "Do you like the music?"

The child's eyes sparked. He withdrew his thumb with a pop. *"Moozika!"*

"Music. Right!" David held out his hand. "Come on, let's go closer so we can watch the dancers."

Stefan grasped David's hand quickly, as if he feared it would be withdrawn. In an instant his budding smile was replaced by a look close to panic.

Did he remember the car accident that had killed his parents? It would be a mercy if he didn't. As far as David knew, Stefan had never spoken of it to anyone. Whatever he had seen had made him run so far from the crash that the police hadn't found him until the next day. The event had traumatized him to the extent that he hadn't uttered a word until his fifth week at the orphanage. Even now he seldom talked.

David sat back on his heels and brushed the hair from Stefan's forehead. That solemn, too-old gaze locked with his, and for an instant, David felt as if he looked back in time at an image of himself thirty years ago.

He didn't need to speak the same language to understand exactly how this boy felt. He knew what it meant to be alone and powerless among strangers, trying to be brave and tough but wishing with every fiber of his being for a place to belong, to be safe, and most of all for someone to love him....

He knew in his heart he would be a good parent to Stefan. It was why he had never considered halting the adoption process after Ellie had left him. He hadn't balked when he'd learned of the recent claim by Stefan's spinster aunt, either; the absentee relative had shown up too late for her case to be considered. The adoption was meant to be. He and this child already shared a bond that went deeper than paperwork or legalities.

A seagull screeched overhead, making Stefan start and press closer to David.

"That's my boy," David murmured. He swallowed hard, struck by the simple truth of what he had just said.

That's my boy.

"I CAN'T BE PATIENT, RUDOLPH. I'm not going to stand by and watch my nephew get ripped from his country and his roots to live on the other side of the world."

Rudolph hissed out a slow breath. "Marina, I don't like the sound of that. What are you planning?"

"I'm going to talk some sense into this American kidnapper."

"No. Absolutely not. No offence, but diplomacy is not your strong suit."

"Diplomacy be damned. Their ship's due to sail at five o'clock."

"Then you wouldn't have an opportunity to speak with him even if his lawyer agreed to a meeting."

"I'll have ten days of opportunities, Rudolph, since I plan to be on board that ship."

* * * * *

Follow Marina and David as they join forces to uncover the reason behind little Stefan's unusual silence, and the secret behind the death of his parents....

Look for From Russia, With Love
*by Ingrid Weaver
in stores June 2007.*

HARLEQUIN®

Mediterranean NIGHTS™

Tycoon Elias Stamos is launching his newest luxury cruise ship from his home port in Greece. But someone from his past is eager to expose old secrets and to see the Stamos empire crumble.

Mediterranean Nights
launches in June 2007 with...

FROM RUSSIA, WITH LOVE
by *Ingrid Weaver*

Join the guests and crew of *Alexandra's Dream* as they are drawn into a world of glamour, romance and intrigue in this new 12-book series.

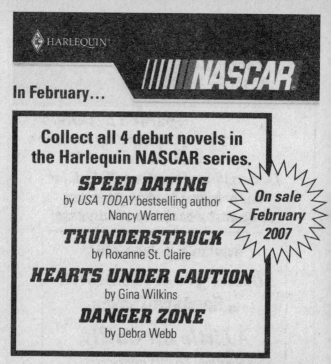

REQUEST YOUR FREE BOOKS!

2 FREE NOVELS PLUS 2 FREE GIFTS!

HARLEQUIN®

Blaze

Red-hot reads!

YES! Please send me 2 FREE Harlequin® Blaze® novels and my 2 FREE gifts. After receiving them, if I don't wish to receive any more books, I can return the shipping statement marked "cancel." If I don't cancel, I will receive 6 brand-new novels every month and be billed just $3.99 per book in the U.S., or $4.47 per book in Canada, plus 25¢ shipping and handling per book and applicable taxes, if any*. That's a savings of at least 15% off the cover price! I understand that accepting the 2 free books and gifts places me under no obligation to buy anything. I can always return a shipment and cancel at any time. Even if I never buy another book from Harlequin, the two free books and gifts are mine to keep forever.

151 HDN EF3W   351 HDN EF3X

Name	(PLEASE PRINT)
Address	Apt.
City	State/Prov.	Zip/Postal Code

Signature (if under 18, a parent or guardian must sign)

Mail to the **Harlequin Reader Service®**:
IN U.S.A.: P.O. Box 1867, Buffalo, NY 14240-1867
IN CANADA: P.O. Box 609, Fort Erie, Ontario L2A 5X3

Not valid to current Harlequin Blaze subscribers.

Want to try two free books from another line?
Call 1-800-873-8635 or visit www.morefreebooks.com.

* Terms and prices subject to change without notice. NY residents add applicable sales tax. Canadian residents will be charged applicable provincial taxes and GST. This offer is limited to one order per household. All orders subject to approval. Credit or debit balances in a customer's account(s) may be offset by any other outstanding balance owed by or to the customer. Please allow 4 to 6 weeks for delivery.

Your Privacy: Harlequin is committed to protecting your privacy. Our Privacy Policy is available online at www.eHarlequin.com or upon request from the Reader Service. From time to time we make our lists of customers available to reputable firms who may have a product or service of interest to you. If you would prefer we not share your name and address, please check here. ☐

HB07

HARLEQUIN®
Super Romance®

Acclaimed author
Brenda Novak
returns to Dundee, Idaho, with

COULDA BEEN A COWBOY

After gaining custody of his infant son,
professional athlete Tyson Garnier hopes to escape
the media and find some privacy in Dundee, Idaho.
He also finds Dakota Brown. But is she ready for the
potential drama that comes with him?

Also watch for:

BLAME IT ON THE DOG by Amy Frazier
(Singles...with Kids)

HIS PERFECT WOMAN by Kay Stockham

DAD FOR LIFE by Helen Brenna
(A Little Secret)

MR. IRRESISTIBLE by Karina Bliss

WANTED MAN by Ellen K. Hartman

Available June 2007 wherever Harlequin books are sold!

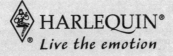

HARLEQUIN®
Live the emotion

HARLEQUIN®

Blaze ™

COMING NEXT MONTH

#327 RISKING IT ALL Stephanie Tyler
Going to the Xtreme: Bigger, Faster, Better is not only the title of Rita Calhoun's hot new documentary, but it's what happens when she falls for one of the film's subjects, undercover navy SEAL John Cashman—the bad boy who's very, very good....

#328 CALL ME WICKED Jamie Sobrato
Extreme
Being a witch isn't easy. Just ask Lauren Parish. She's on the run from witch-hunters with a hot guy she's forbidden to touch. Worse, she's had Carson McCullen and knows *exactly* how good he is. Maybe it's time to be completely wicked and forget all the rules.

#329 SHADOW HAWK Jill Shalvis
ATF agent Abby Wells might be madly in lust with gorgeous fellow agent JT Hawk, but she's not about to do something stupid. Then again, walking into the middle of a job gone wrong—*and* getting herself kidnapped by Hawk—isn't the smartest thing she's ever done. Still, she's not about to make matters worse by sleeping with him. *Is she?*

#330 THE P.I. Cara Summers
Tall, Dark...and Dangerously Hot! Bk. 1
Writer-slash-sleuth Kit Angelis is living a *noir* novel: a gorgeous blonde walks into his office, covered in blood, carrying a wad of cash and a gun and has no idea who she is. She's also sexy as hell, which is making it hard for Kit to keep his mind on the mystery....

#331 NO RULES Shannon Hollis
Are the Laws of Seduction the latest fad for a guy to snag a sexy date, or a blueprint for murder? Policewoman Joanna MacPherson needs to find out. Posing as a lonely single, she and her partner, sexy Cooper Maxwell, play a dangerous game of cat and mouse that might uncover a lot more than they bargained for....

#332 ONE NIGHT STANDARDS Cathy Yardley
A flight gone awry and a road trip from hell turn into the night that never seems to end for Sophie Jones and Mark McMann. But the starry sky and combustible sexual heat between the two of them say they won't be complaining.... In fact, it may just be the trip of a lifetime!

www.eHarlequin.com

HBCNM0507